TENDER
GUARDIAN

*Also by Cathie Linz
in Large Print:*

One of a Kind Marriage
Wildfire

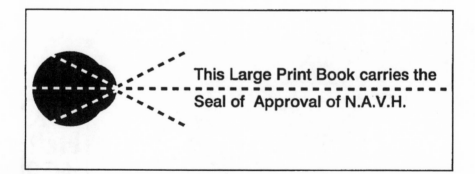

This Large Print Book carries the
Seal of Approval of N.A.V.H.

TENDER GUARDIAN

Cathie Linz

G.K. Hall & Co.
Thorndike, Maine

Published in 1996 by arrangement with Cathie Linz.

G.K. Hall Large Print Romance Collection.

The text of this Large Print edition is unabridged.
Other aspects of the book may vary from the original edition.

Set in 16 pt. Bookman Old Style by Minnie B. Raven.

Printed in the United States on permanent paper.

Library of Congress Cataloging in Publication Data:

Linz, Cathie.
   Tender guardian / Cathie Linz.
     p.   cm.
   ISBN 0-7838-1909-9 (lg. print : hc)
   1. Large type books. I. Title.
  [PS3562.I558T46   1996]
   813'.54—dc20   96-31686

Special thanks to Diane Alice
for the generous sharing of
her teaching experience
and numerous "kids' stories."
Hawshaw!

CHAPTER ONE

Ray Lewis swallowed the last of his antacid tablet. In all his years in sales he'd never run across a case that had disturbed his ulcer more than this one had. Taking a deep breath, Ray valiantly broke the bad news to his boss. "We've got more trouble with the Percival School account. Brittany Evans has turned down another applicant."

Michael Devlin, the thirty-year-old founder and president of Security Management Systems, did not look pleased. Michael had carefully built his company's reputation into that of an up-and-coming supplier of security guards in the state of Maryland; he did not appreciate having that reputation blotted by a feisty kindergarten director. "I hand-picked that last applicant myself!"

Ray sank into the nearest chair. "I know."

"What was the problem this time?" Michael voiced the question with what he considered to be fatalistic resignation.

"According to Ms. Evans, and I'm quoting, 'The man did not have a temperament suitable for working with children.' End of quote."

Michael's retort was sharply sarcastic. "The man's got five kids of his own, what more does she want?"

"I wish I knew," Ray murmured.

Michael made a concerted effort to hang on to his temper. He rarely lost it and was reputed to have an unshakable calm. "Something's got to be done about this Evans woman. Have you tried talking to her?"

Ray nodded wearily.

"And?"

"I didn't get anywhere."

"She must be a tough nut to crack if you can't get through to her." The terse statement was Michael's way of stating his confidence in Ray's sales abilities.

But Ray had more bad news to deliver. "She's threatening to cancel our security contract with the school if we don't deliver an acceptable security guard by noon today."

Michael received the news with a muttered curse. "We are not going to lose this account." Ever since Sam, the Percival School's original guard, had been forced to move away unexpectedly owing to his wife's ill health, the search for a suitable replacement had grown into a challenge for Michael. And everyone knew that Michael Devlin never walked away from a challenge, or let it walk away from him. "Hell, how

8

hard can it be to find one security guard for an elite kindergarten? We've handled jobs far tougher than this one."

"But none more frustrating," Ray inserted.

"You got that right." Michael leaned back in his office chair. "She's already cost me one damn good security guard, Bruno Maretti. We still don't know what happened to make him leave, do we?"

Ray shook his head. "After working at Percival School for one day, Bruno came back here and simply handed in his notice. No explanations given. Rumor is that he's left the security field entirely. I believe he's selling shoes now."

"What about Johnny?" Michael asked, naming the second security guard hired to work at the school. "Did he say anything?"

"Just that he'd do *anything* rather than be sent back to that school."

"These are competent men, able to take care of themselves in any situation. We're talking about guys who have dealt with riots and robbery attempts without blinking an eye. Yet send them to the Percival School and they turn into mush!" Michael shook his head in amazement. "What can she be doing to them?"

"I wish I knew. One thing's for sure, Brittany Evans is definitely hard to please. According to her, all of our subsequent

9

applicants have been either too old, too young, too fierce —"

"Too fierce!" Michael objected. "Give me the file."

Ray obeyed the curt command. "What are you going to do?"

"I'm going to take the next applicant's place this morning and pay Brittany Evans a little visit myself."

Standing in her classroom with her hands on her hips, Brittany Evans raised her voice in anger. "Come back here!"

Harvey, the rabbit, ignored the authoritative order and continued his scampering flight. Across the floor of Percival School's classroom he hopped, intent on reaching an open window and indulging his case of spring fever.

"No, don't go that way!" Brittany swooped down to scoop up the escapee, but not before Harvey had hopped across the still-wet sign she'd just painted.

Harvey did not appreciate having his merry romp curtailed and he made another wiggling bid for freedom. Brittany hung on to the classroom pet and eventually won the brief tussle. Her baggy T-shirt, however, showed marked signs of the battle. A dozen purple and red paw prints now ran across the sky-blue cotton material in a haphazard path from her shoulder to her navel.

Harvey had added several more Technicolor paw prints to Brittany's bare arms by the time she'd carried him over to a small stainless sink in the far corner of the classroom and began briskly washing off his paws. At least the paint was water-soluble, although the disgruntled rabbit showed little appreciation of that fact.

"Listen, Harvey, consider yourself lucky that the kids are still on spring break." Brittany shook her head at the mental image of a pack of eager four- and five-year-olds chasing Harvey around the classroom. Harvey also looked distressed at the thought.

After drying the rabbit's paws with a paper towel, she proclaimed, "There, you're as good as new. I hope you've learned your lesson," Brittany scolded in her best teacher's voice. The rabbit twitched his ears in what Brittany took to be an affirmative response. "Good. Now I've got to get ready to meet another job applicant, so it's back in your cage for you. . . ."

Brittany had barely closed the cage latch when she heard a deep male voice from across the room. "Excuse me . . ."

She jumped in surprise and pivoted to face him.

Michael's eyes narrowed briefly as he observed the young woman's paint-splattered appearance. His gaze slid over her, from the

11

top of her short hair to the tips of her bare feet as they peeked out from the cuffs of her baggy jeans.

Frowning in confusion, Michael said, "I'm looking for Brittany Evans."

Oh, no! Surely it wasn't ten-thirty already? Brittany's startled gaze flew to her wrist, where she not only discovered that her watch had stopped but also noted the colorful paw prints still adorning her arms. Gathering up a handful of fresh paper towels, she began speaking while briskly wiping off the worst stains. "I apologize for my appearance, Mr. Devlin. It is Mr. Devlin, isn't it?" As far as she remembered that was the name the representative of Security Management Systems had given her over the phone when they'd set up this interview earlier this morning. But then there had been so many applicants, it was becoming hard to keep them straight.

"I'm Michael Devlin," the man verified before asking, "You're the director of this school?"

She thought his voice expressed an inordinate amount of disbelief. "That's right." She saw no point in discussing the interim nature of her directorship. This was not the time to go into details, not dressed as she was. "I'm Brittany Evans. And as I said before, I apologize for my appearance. Unfortunately, Harvey decided to assert his independence and paint the town red this morning." Since the paper towel wasn't doing much good, Brittany threw the wadded mess in the trash can.

"Who's Harvey?" Michael looked around as if expecting to see another paint-spattered figure lurking somewhere in the room.

"Harvey is our rabbit," she explained.

"I see."

Brittany edged her way toward the doorway. "Yes, well, if you don't mind waiting here a few minutes, I'll just go clean up and then we can begin the interview."

Keeping a smile in place, she exited before Michael Devlin could reply, leaving him standing in the middle of the classroom.

Even after her departure Michael kept staring at the doorway through which she'd disappeared. Brittany Evans? That sexy lady? He shook his head. She didn't fit his expectations at all. He'd anticipated something more along the lines of orthopedic shoes and military precision, not bare feet and big blue eyes.

In the privacy of the staff bathroom Brittany's smile had been replaced by the type of grimace her four-year-old students wore when things weren't going their way.

"Talk about inauspicious beginnings . . ." She ruefully shook her head at her mirrored reflection.

Intent on making up the ground she felt

13

she'd lost, Brittany efficiently washed up before peeling off her T-shirt and jeans. The simple Laura Ashley dress she'd meant to wear for the interview was already hanging on the back of the bathroom door where she'd put it upon arriving at the school earlier this morning. The outfit was perfect for the lovely day in early April, but inappropriate for the chores of sign painting and animal feeding she'd had to complete first, thus her T-shirt and jeans.

After smoothing the dress over her head, she zipped up the back with a supple contortion made easier by her double-jointed flexibility, one of the few traits her father had bestowed upon her. Brittany's chestnut hair, with its varying copper and gold highlights, could be traced directly to her mother, although Charlene Evans would never dream of wearing her hair this short.

Brittany liked being able to finger-comb the style back into shape, exactly as her hairdresser, Jean-Pierre, had taught her to do. And he was right, the look worked for her. If only it were as easy to find a suitable security guard to work for her!

"They just don't make guards like they used to." Having made that proclamation, she pulled on a pair of stockings and hurriedly slid her feet into a pair of flat shoes that matched the briar-rose color of the dress.

Brittany found Michael Devlin studying a bulletin-board display of her students' artwork when she returned to the classroom. He turned to face her before she'd made a sound.

Brittany had been too concerned about her own disheveled appearance to notice Michael Devlin's before, so now she took a moment to take stock of this latest applicant. He was tall but not overpoweringly so — about six feet, give or take a half inch. His light-brown sun-streaked hair fell over his forehead without getting into his eyes.

Brittany's attention focused on those masculine eyes. While too far away to note their color, she was struck by an inscrutability of expression that told her a lot about Michael Devlin. She mentally classified him as the strong and silent type, the kind of man who revealed little of his experiences.

As her eyes slipped past the unbuttoned collar of his blue shirt and traveled over the breadth of his chest, she had to admit to feeling a momentary twinge of intimidation at the harnessed power he projected. Although his muscular upper torso matched that of many a professional football player, the leanness of his hips and long legs made him brawny rather than burly. The long sleeves of his shirt were rolled up to reveal arms that were sinewy and supple, with a tan darker than the one Brittany had from

15

a winter trip to Florida. Michael Devlin might be too aggressively male for her own tastes, but he certainly did make a physical impact.

He intensified that impact by spreading his arms and legs so she could get a better look. "Well, do I pass inspection?"

Not one to be embarrassed easily, Brittany shot back, "I won't know until I've checked your résumé."

"I've got it right here," Michael told her, reaching into his back pocket to pull out a folded envelope and hand it to her.

The papers inside were warm. Brittany's fingers registered that fact as she unfolded the sheets.

Michael shifted his attention away from the woman standing before him, because had he not done so he was liable to say something he shouldn't. The darkly intimate direction of his thoughts surprised him. Hoping to detour his mind from temptation, Michael made a stab at polite conversation. "This is some zoo you've got here."

Brittany glanced up from the pages she was studying. "Not quite a zoo," she murmured, a little absently. "Just a garden snake, a spider, a lizard, a guinea pig, a rabbit, two hamsters, an ant farm, and a tankful of fish."

"What's all this junk in the spider's case?"

Brittany moved closer to peer into the small glass terrarium housing the spider. "That's Munch's jungle gym. The kids name all the animals," she parenthetically added. "They named the spider Munch and made that jungle gym out of Popsicle sticks so that Munch would have something to weave his web around."

Michael was concentrating more on the light floral scent of Brittany's perfume than on the content of her words. Standing so close beside her, he couldn't help but notice that the top of her head would just about reach his chin were he to hold her in his arms. He also noticed the way her dress complemented her curves: the thrust of her breasts, the flair of her hips. His inflection was uncharacteristically distracted as he voiced his thoughts. "This doesn't bother you?" Whatever this was, it sure as hell bothered him.

"What doesn't bother me?" Brittany's forehead wrinkled in confusion.

"The spider," he lied.

"I can't afford to be bothered. The kids are constantly walking up to me and handing me all kinds of things to look at. It would be very unprofessional of me to scream and run." Turning to face him, she caught the beginning signs of a smile on his lips and was startled by the flash of attraction she felt. Retreating to a safer distance, she spoke with sudden formality. "If you'll come into the office, we can complete the interview there."

The only good reason Brittany had for choosing the office over the classroom was that the former boasted a desk and Brittany suddenly felt the need to place a barrier, even if it was only an old oak desk, between herself and Michael Devlin. Once she was seated, she spread out the two pages of Michael's résumé on the desktop.

Michael, meanwhile, had settled himself into the chair across from her and was quietly studying her.

"You come highly recommended." Brittany's voice reflected none of the nervousness she was experiencing at being the center of Michael's studious attention.

"Thanks."

How did he manage to infuse so much into one small word? Brittany wasn't sure how he'd done it, but somehow Michael had managed to make her feel as if she'd just complimented him on a very personal rather than a strictly professional level.

"I see you've worked for Security Management Systems for some time."

"Since the beginning," Michael laconically supplied.

"I also see you've completed such exciting assignments as handling security at several rock concerts and acting as a bodyguard for an oil sheikh's family," she noted, referring to just a few of his previous assignments as they'd been listed on his résumé. "I'm impressed, Mr. Devlin, but I'm also curious." She leaned back in her chair and fixed him with a direct stare. "Why would a man with your experience choose to look after a group of four- and five-year-old children?"

"As you said, my last few jobs were pretty exciting, at times too exciting. I felt the need for a change."

"I wouldn't exactly call this job peaceful," she warned him. "We've got thirty children here, all of them between the ages of four and five. The noise level can get deafening at times. And if you're unaccustomed to children, their antics can be nerve-racking."

"My nerves are pretty sturdy." Michael leaned back in his chair, his legs stretched out before him. "As for kids, I grew up with a lot of them."

"You come from a large family?"

"Six brothers and sisters."

Brittany noted that fact on the margin of his résumé before asking, "You have no children of your own?"

"No. Do you?"

She looked surprised by his question. "No."

"Not married, huh?" His gaze intentionally

19

lingered on the bare ring finger of her left hand.

"Not that it makes the slightest bit of difference, but no, I'm not married, Mr. Devlin."

"Me, neither." Michael found himself smiling at the way Brittany eyed him with haughty disapproval. No doubt about it, Brittany Evans oozed class. Even her name sounded rich.

Brittany chose to overlook his comment. "I don't know how much you were told about our requirements here . . ."

"The only thing I've heard is that you're very choosy."

Again he made the observation sound as if he were referring to personal rather than business matters.

"That's true, I am extremely choosy, but how did you come to hear about it?" Her blue eyes narrowed suspiciously.

"There's no need to get het up," he assured her. "I didn't see it written on the walls of a phone booth above your phone number."

"What a relief."

Her sarcasm rolled right off him. "You've built yourself quite a reputation, you know."

"No, I didn't know, but I have a feeling you're about to enlighten me."

"The guys have concocted quite a few

stories about you."

The news made Brittany frown. "What guys?"

"The other security guards." Michael's expression remained formal, but there was a surprising glimpse of boyish humor in his watchful eyes. "Anyone who goes through men the way you do is bound to be talked about."

"By men, I presume you are talking about security guards?"

"Of course." He nodded with grave mockery.

"Of course." Her voice was equally grave, and even more mocking. "I wouldn't have thought our needs were that unusual here."

"I'm sure your needs are very normal."

"I was referring to the school's security needs, Mr. Devlin, not my own."

The tilt of his head was apologetic. "I didn't intend to be personal." To which he silently tacked on, *Not yet, anyway!*

"I'm glad to hear that. After all, should you get this job, I would in effect be your boss, Mr. Devlin. And it's never wise to alienate the boss."

Michael hid his surprise. The idea of a client considering herself to be the boss was new to him. "I would never dream of alienating you, Ms. Evans." That much was true. Seduction, not alienation, was on his mind.

"To get back to the school's security

needs, most of our students come from prominent families here in Annapolis. Several are the daughters and sons of state senators and representatives."

Michael tried to look suitably impressed. Annapolis was the capital of the state of Maryland, so it stood to reason that the politicians would send their kids to a fancy private school.

"Basically we need a guard during the day to discourage any possible kidnapping attempts. We've already had a security system installed to deter any burglary attempts after-hours."

"Have you had any trouble before?"

"We did have one burglary before the new system was installed. And last year we had some trouble concerning a case of child custody. A student's father attempted to take his son from school, but Sam handled the situation. Sam was our last permanent security guard," Brittany explained. "He worked here for five years. Unfortunately, he had to move to Arizona last month, because of his wife's poor health. Before he left we tried to break in a new security guard."

"What happened?" Michael asked, as if he didn't already know.

"Two quit; one was dismissed."

Ah, here was his chance to pick up some information. "Why did you dismiss the guy?"

Brittany's reply was cool. "He had trouble taking orders from a woman."

Michael's jaw tightened, the only visible sign of his displeasure. "That's it?"

"That's all you need to know, Mr. Devlin. I hope I won't encounter the same difficulty with you?"

Before Michael could douse his inner anger sufficiently to reply, Brittany threw more fuel on the fire.

"You are younger than I had hoped. Only thirty." She frowned while absently tapping a finger against his résumé. "I feel the children relate better to a more mature male figure, like Sam. He was in his late fifties."

"My age makes you feel uncomfortable?" There was an underlying challenge in his question.

"Not at all, Mr. Devlin." She met his challenge, and his stare, head on. "Do you have any other questions?"

Michael eyed her with a well-hidden glint of amusement. "About the job?"

"Of course about the job."

"In that case, what are the hours?"

"From eight-fifteen until four-fifteen, with a half hour off for lunch."

"Who watches the kids then?"

"The teaching assistants."

"My uniform . . . ?"

"Will be jeans and a Percival School T-shirt,"

Brittany inserted. "I don't want the children to be frightened of you. A security guard's uniform would intimidate them."

"What about a gun?"

"You may lock it in the office safe, that's where Sam left his. With the children, we can't take the risk of having a gun around."

Michael was beginning to understand why his guards had thrown in the towel. Brittany Evans was stubborn as hell. Bossy, too. "A gun isn't going to do much good locked in a safe should it be needed," he pointed out with barely restrained impatience.

"If it's needed, you may take it out of the safe, Mr. Devlin."

"Right." His satirical inflection told her what he thought of that idea.

"Your employment records indicate that you're an expert in some form of martial arts. Is that correct?"

"Yes."

"Then you'll have that to fall back on should a dangerous situation arise." Having stated her views, Brittany proceeded briskly to change the subject. "Because of your lack of experience with children we'll have to try you on a probationary period of . . . say . . . two weeks."

"You're offering me the job?"

"If you want it under the conditions I've

24

specified, then yes, you have the job. Are you interested?"

"Oh, I'm definitely interested."

Luckily Brittany's eyes were on the notes she was making and not on her newly hired security guard, or she would have seen the unmistakably predatory look he gave her. As it was she detected no hidden nuances in his voice.

"In that case, the job is yours. I don't mind telling you, Mr. Devlin, that you were Security Management Systems' last chance. Had they not sent someone suitable by noon today, I was going to hire another firm to handle our school's security needs."

"Haven't you heard? Security Management Systems aims to please; we'll do whatever it takes to get the job done." Michael paused a moment before adding a casual postscript. "Even if it means that I, as president of the company, have to handle this job myself."

CHAPTER TWO

The president of Security Management Systems?" At his nod, Brittany angrily continued: "Why the subterfuge, Mr. Devlin?"

Michael countered her question with one of his own. "Why the anger, Ms. Evans? You delivered an ultimatum, we delivered an acceptable guard for your school."

"Yourself?"

He nodded. "For the time being."

"What does that mean?"

"It means that until we can find this perfect guard with all the requirements you demand, I will fill the vacancy."

Brittany was obviously displeased with the idea. "I'm tired of having temporary employees handling our security needs. I want someone on a more permanent basis."

Michael suspected Brittany's comment reflected her feelings about her own needs as well. Brittany Evans wasn't the type of woman to indulge in a wild affair, but that didn't prevent him from imagining her in bed with him. His voice reflected some measure of satisfaction as he said, "Your school's security needs will be met." He intended fulfilling her more intimate needs himself.

"Why is your company having so much trouble finding us a guard? I never anticipated it would take so long to fill this position."

"As I said before, your employee requirements are rather specific." The disbelieving tilt of her chin prompted him to add, "It's hard finding a security guard who isn't too fierce."

Brittany returned his taunt with one of her own. "Your company found Sam for us and we kept him for five years. Apparently at one time you were able to find personnel that wasn't too fierce. I hope you haven't lost the knack? I also hope you realize, Mr. Devlin, that regardless of your lofty position with Security Management Systems, here at Percival School you will have to take orders from me."

"You seem to have a thing about giving orders," Michael noted in a quiet voice. "Why is that?"

"I'm merely clarifying our positions."

He appeared amused by her superior attitude. "You, boss lady, me, measly guard, is that right?"

"I'm the interim director of this school and as such —"

"Interim director? Why interim?"

Brittany silently cursed her unintentional

slip. Maintaining control over Michael Devlin was going to be difficult enough without the added handicap of her provisional position. "The school's owner and director, Doris Carlyle, has taken a year's sabbatical to study child-care facilities in other countries. In her absence she has appointed me as interim director."

"What was your position with the school before you became interim director?"

"I've been the assistant director for three years and I taught here for two years before that."

Michael studied her with speculation in his misty green eyes. "You don't look old enough to have been a teacher for five years."

"I've been a teacher for eight years," Brittany corrected him. "I've worked here for five."

"But that would make you . . ."

"Twenty-nine. So don't let my looks fool you, Mr. Devlin. I am more than capable of running this school." Her tone was intentionally brisk.

"Is there a policy against using first names here?"

She blinked at the sudden change of subject. "No . . ."

"Then I'm Michael. And you're Brittany."

She accepted his proclamation with a shrug. The usage of her name wasn't an issue worth arguing about. Brittany had a feeling that there would be plenty of other battles more deserving.

"So, Brittany, if you've got the time, I'd appreciate a brief tour of the school so I can get an idea of the layout."

"Fine." She was pleased to see this example of professionalism. She led Michael out of the office. "The school only has one main entrance, and two fire exits that activate an alarm when opened. This is the guard's desk here" — she gestured to a simple wooden desk that sat right outside her office. "From this position in the front hallway you can see everyone who enters or exits from any of these doorways."

"Okay, I know that's the front door" — he pointed straight ahead — "and this door" — he gestured to his left — "leads to a classroom. Your office is behind us, so where do these other two doors lead?"

Brittany walked over to open the one on the other side of the guard's desk. "This is the kitchen —"

"Kitchen!" Michael glanced over her shoulder to confirm her words.

"You sound surprised."

"I am. My kindergarten never had a kitchen at its disposal."

"It's not exactly a luxury," Brittany retorted, stung by the implied criticism in his mocking voice. "The children do a number of cooking exercises over the course of the year. On special occasions, like Parents' Day, they even prepare an entire meal themselves. The teachers and teaching aides eat their lunches in here as well."

"Right."

Brittany closed the kitchen door with a decided bang and moved on to the next door. "This is our second classroom, laid out exactly as the one across the hall."

"Where you and Harvey were painting the town red."

Borrowing an expression from him, she smiled sweetly and murmured, "Right. And that's the end of the tour. So if you have no more questions, Michael, I'll see you at eight-fifteen on Monday morning."

"How'd it go?" Ray Lewis asked Michael the moment he returned to Security Management Systems' office.

"We've got the job," Michael announced with a wide smile.

"How about taking your secretary out to lunch to celebrate?" Arlene Antosiak suggested.

"I might be tempted if my secretary didn't religiously go home for lunch every day because she can't stand to be parted from her beloved husband. And at your age, too, Arlene." Michael shook his head, grinning at the mutinous flush on Arlene's face.

"You just wait till the love bug bites you. Then we'll see who laughs last. And fifty-two is not old," she added as Michael grabbed his messages off her desk and waved Ray on into his office.

Ray sank into the same chair from which he'd had to deliver bad news earlier that morning. "How'd you manage this miracle with Percival School?"

"By promising to fill the job myself until we came up with the ideal candidate."

"That's an innovative approach."

"Desperation is the mother of invention," Michael misquoted wryly.

"Did Brittany Evans give you any trouble?"

Michael tossed aside his messages and mildly questioned, "Aside from stirring up my hormones, you mean?"

Ray's mouth dropped open. "You found her attractive?"

Michael laughed. "By the doubt I hear in your voice, I take it that you've never met the lady yourself?"

"No, our encounters have all been over the phone."

"She's not what I expected." Michael made the admission in an unusually soft voice.

"Tell me more."

Ray's eager words brought Michael out of his dreamworld. "On a scale of one to ten?"

Ray nodded.

31

"I'd give her a twenty-five." Ray groaned with masculine envy. "But she's bossy as hell," Michael added.

"Sounds interesting."

Michael nodded, an anticipatory smile curving his lips. "She is."

Brittany might have been pleased at having been described as interesting, but she would have counted the twenty-five Michael quoted as being severely inflated. As she prepared for work early Monday morning she found herself pausing in front of her full-length mirror and viewing herself with a critical eye. Normally she liked these olive-green trousers and this contrasting pink shirt. But today she felt strangely restless.

Turning away from the mirror, she told herself that it was natural, having turned twenty-nine only last week, that she should be worrying more about her appearance. Post-birthday paranoia. Logically she knew her thighs weren't really any heavier, her stomach any less flat, but nonetheless she frowned and replaced her bagged lunch with a single carton of yogurt.

Brittany was storing her single carton of lemon yogurt in the compact-size refrigerator in the school's kitchen when Michael again managed to approach her from behind, his step undetected.

"Nice," he murmured approvingly.

Brittany straightened and swiveled to face him. The look in his eyes made her voice unintentionally defensive. "What's nice?"

"The refrigerator." Michael's frankly appraising gaze lifted from the vicinity of her hips to meet the fire in her blue eyes. "I've got one of those little models in my apartment."

She was well aware that he had not been looking at the compact appliance, but decided challenging him would be pointless. "You're here early, Mr. Devlin. It's only seven forty-five."

"Are you like this every morning?"

"Like what?"

"Formal. Want some coffee?"

She gestured toward the space-saving automatic coffee brewer hanging from beneath the kitchen cabinets. "It isn't made yet."

Michael lifted the white paper bag he was carrying. "Two cups of coffee and two hot apple fritters. Interested?"

Brittany paused, clearly tempted. Her breakfast had consisted of orange juice and a half grapefruit; full of vitamin C, but not very satisfying.

"The fritters are fresh," he added in a persuasive voice. Seeing her still wavering, he added one final clincher. "If you don't eat one, I'll throw it away."

The thought of such waste made up her

mind. "In that case, I will have one, thank you."

"Good." Michael opened the bag and handed her a paper-wrapped fritter.

She sat down, expecting him to join her. And so he did, but in his own way. Michael grabbed a kitchen chair and reversed it so the seat was facing away from the table. Slinging one leg over the plastic-covered seat, he then sat down and rested an arm on the chair's back. In between sipping coffee and munching on a flaky apple fritter, Michael said, "Tell me about the school."

"Could you be a little more specific? What in particular would you like to know about the school? The building, the curriculum, the staff?"

"Start with the building and then go on to the other two. What was this originally, a warehouse?"

"Excellent guess. It was indeed a warehouse. Its location near Annapolis's residential neighborhoods made it the perfect place for a kindergarten. Because the building sits sideways to the street, we even had room to build a good-sized playground."

"Mmm" — Michael swallowed the last of his apple fritter — "go on."

"Doris converted it into a school in the late sixties. She decided to gear the curriculum toward four- and five-year-olds, preschool and kindergarten age, because she felt and still feels that children learn so much in that period of their development. As far as staff is concerned, aside from myself we have one other full-time teacher and one part-time teacher who works afternoons. We also have four teaching assistants, two for each class."

As if on cue, Brittany's two teaching assistants came into the kitchen amid a flurry of cheerful chatter. The two women carpooled, so they always arrived together. They stopped when they saw Michael.

"I'm sorry," Joan Shelding apologized. "We didn't know you were busy, Britt."

"That's okay. I'd like you to meet our new security guard, Michael Devlin. Michael, this is Joan Shelding, one of my teaching assistants." Michael stood up and Brittany waited until he had finished shaking Joan's hand before continuing her introductions. "And this is Marcia Winston, another teaching assistant."

After shaking Marcia's hand, Michael stepped back and looked at the three women before him. "I can see I'm going to enjoy this job, surrounded by lovely ladies."

Fifty-four, mother of five, and grandmother of four, Joan was thrilled to be included in Michael's gallant statement. Thirty-four and mother of two, Marcia was equally thrilled by the compliment. Only Brittany was not beaming with pleasure.

"Michael will only be working here temporarily until his company can find us someone to fill the job permanently," Brittany explained.

"Your company?" Marcia asked.

"That's right," Michael confirmed.

Before he could go into any more detail, Brittany interrupted him. "It's almost eight-fifteen, Michael. The children's parents begin dropping them off soon and I think it would be best if you kept an eye on their arrival. But before you go out, I'd like you to come into the office and change into a Percival School T-shirt so the parents will know you work for the school."

With a joint "It was nice meeting you," Joan and Marcia proceeded to Brittany's classroom, where they had projects to set up before class began.

Brittany led Michael to the office, where she headed for a metal supply cabinet near the back of the room. Turning with a bright green T-shirt in hand, she found Michael in the process of taking off the blue shirt he had been wearing.

"What are you doing?" she asked, shocked.

"You told me to change." He shrugged, drawing attention to muscles Brittany didn't even know the names of. "So I'm changing."

Brittany was changing, too, internally,

where sudden desires were running free. For one brief second she just stood there, absorbing the almost tangible impact of raw masculine power. Unwillingly her eyes traveled over Michael's bare chest, over the ridge of his collarbone down the rippling expanse of tanned skin to the swirling whorls of golden brown hair that formed an erotic V from his navel down to the waistband of his low-cut jeans.

Taking a deep breath, she reined in her wayward thoughts and resolutely gathered her self-control. Michael's physique may have been admirable, from a strictly impersonal point of view, but he was not her type. She preferred her men leaner and less earthy-looking. Having told herself that, she felt much better. Didn't she?

Michael watched her expressions change with frustrated confusion. For one brief moment he was sure he'd seen a flash of awareness in her eyes, but now it was gone, replaced with a remoteness he found infuriating. "Something wrong, Brittany?"

"Not at all." She handed him the T-shirt. "I was thinking about my class schedule."

Michael knew all was not lost, however, when he caught her unguarded stare as he completed tugging on the T-shirt. Deciding to experiment, he deliberately flexed his pectoral muscles and made the already snug-fitting T-shirt even snugger. When he saw Brittany's eyes widen, he had to re-press a smile of male satisfaction. That look she'd given him had nothing to do with class schedules!

All in all Brittany thought she'd handled things pretty smoothly, keeping her cool until Shelly Neumann, the school's other full-time teacher, bumped into her in the hallway five minutes later and sighed. "Who's that gorgeous man out front? The one with the nifty eyes and the beautiful biceps."

Shelly's description and the dreamy look on her face reaffirmed Brittany's opinion that it was a good thing this particular security guard's tenure would be short. It clearly wouldn't take long for her entire staff to become besotted. "That's Michael Devlin. He's going to be our security guard until a more suitable man can be found."

Shelly smoothed back her nearly waist-length ash-blond hair. "He looks perfectly suitable to me, Britt. Why can't he remain permanently?"

"He's too young." Brittany thought that sounded a bit curt so she added, "The kids relate better to an older man."

"The kids seem to be relating to him fine." Shelly held back the curtain on the front-hall window to prove her point. Indeed a group of children had already clustered around Michael and were apparently bombarding him with questions.

Brittany reached the front door in time to hear an example of one of her students' sense of imagination. "This is our guard," five-year-old Daniel was grandly informing four-year-old Maria. "He's here to make sure we all stay in school." Lowering his voice to a loud whisper, Daniel added, "And he keeps the dinosaurs away."

"I don't like him," Maria muttered to her Cabbage Patch doll.

"That's just cuz you're scared," freckle-faced Kevin taunted.

"Am not," Maria denied.

"You are too."

"Am not!"

"Are too!"

"There's no such thing as dinosaurs." This proclamation came from Matthew, another of Brittany's students. Matthew's parents were both research scientists and had trained their son early on to differentiate between fact and fantasy.

Before Matthew and Daniel could enter into one of their familiar arguments about the reality of dinosaurs, Brittany diverted their attention by formally introducing Michael to them. "This is Mr. Devlin and he is going to be acting as our security guard for the next few weeks."

"Acting? Like on TV?" Daniel asked, his eyes hopeful. "Like a superhero on TV?"

Daniel's sometimes best friend Adam spoke up for the first time to say, "Yeah! Spiderman or Batman!"

"No, Daniel, Adam. By 'acting,' I meant that he is taking the job for a while."

"How come?" The question came from Daniel.

"Because he's got another job he has to go to then," Brittany explained.

"Is he your husband?" Tiffany demanded out of the blue. But then that was Tiffany's specialty, coming up with things out of the blue.

"No."

Tiffany continued her inquisition. "Does he live with you?"

Brittany did not appreciate the way Michael was grinning. He was obviously enjoying the situation. After tossing him a reprimanding look, she directed her attention back to Tiffany. "No, Tiffany, he does not live with me."

"Why not? You're a couple, and it would be so romantic."

Romantic was Tiffany's favorite adjective; she was forever instructing her fellow classmates to be more romantic.

"Michael and I are not a couple, Tiffany. We work together, that's all. Just like Sam and I worked together. You all remember Sam, don't you?"

The children all nodded, except for Maria,

who clutched her doll even tighter and continued eying Michael with marked distrust.

Meanwhile, Tiffany was not about to give up. "Sam was *tooooo* old. That wouldn't have been romantic, to live with him."

"Maybe Michael has a wife at home," practical Matthew pointed out.

"Do you?" Tiffany asked Michael.

"No, I'm not married," Michael answered.

Tiffany turned to the rest of the children with a triumphant expression. "There, see!"

Michael's presence was a prime topic of discussion in Brittany's kindergarten class throughout the morning. Usually the children were easier to handle in small groups of five or so with either Brittany, Joan, or Marcia supervising things. Activities were rotated so everyone got a chance at doing artwork, experimenting at the science table, and story-dictating, to name a few. Story-dictating was a particular class favorite.

But today the children's attention remained focused on the school's new, albeit temporary, security guard. In her art group Tiffany painted a picture of Michael. During story-dictating Daniel incorporated Michael into his latest dinosaur saga. Even Maria referred to Michael while playing in the doll corner, inauspiciously renaming the villainous Darth Vader doll Michael.

With the kids being particularly rambunctious Brittany didn't get a chance to introduce Michael to Shelly. However, when Shelly and Michael joined her in the kitchen at twelve-thirty, Brittany realized that the two had obviously handled the introductions themselves. Brittany also realized that Shelly was looking at Michael as if she'd like to devour him for lunch.

"Really, Britt won't mind," Shelly was huskily assuring Michael in a voice more suitable for a fifteen-year-old groupie than a twenty-five-year-old woman. "After all you are entitled to a lunch break. I know you said you didn't bring anything with you but like I said, I've more than enough quiche to share."

Quiche? No way could Brittany see Michael Devlin sitting down to eat quiche. But down he sat. Right next to her.

"How was your morning?" he asked Brittany with polite interest.

"Fine. And yours?" Her tone was managerial.

"No problems."

Shelly popped her famous quiche into the microwave and minutes later removed the warmed food, setting a dish in front of Michael with an inviting smile.

When Michael's smile matched Shelly's in warmth Brittany vigorously dug her spoon into her carton of yogurt. Shelly and Michael seemed unaware of her darkening disposition as they exchanged flirtatious quips and meaningful glances. After watching them for twenty minutes Brittany couldn't stomach any more.

She tossed her half-full carton of yogurt into the trash and left without a word, certain that her absence would not be noticed.

"Something seems to be bothering your boss," Michael noted with a certain amount of satisfaction.

"I hadn't noticed," Shelly murmured.

Michael briefly wondered why he felt nothing for Shelly Neumann. She was a beautiful woman and she would obviously be receptive. Had he not met Brittany first, he no doubt would have been interested. But as it was, Brittany's impression left no room for anyone else in his mind. However, Michael was not above using a little jealousy to help his cause along. And judging by Brittany's unexplained early departure a few moments ago, his tactics appeared to be working.

Brittany remained closeted in her office for the remainder of the afternoon, emerging only long enough to briefly introduce Michael to Ann Bedford, the part-time teacher who worked afternoons. The morning's students were replaced with the afternoon shift, but now Ann was teaching in what Michael had already begun to consider *Brittany's* classroom.

By four-fifteen the children had all departed, picked up by welcoming parents. Michael wiled away some time talking to Shelly, or more specifically listening to her talking, until everyone had left except for Brittany. As soon as Shelly had departed he went in search of Brittany.

He found her in her classroom, setting out some sort of display in what appeared to be the storytelling corner, judging by the low-built bookcases and comfy-looking chair.

Instinct told him that Brittany was aware of his presence but she made no effort to acknowledge it until he asked, "Need some help?"

"No, thanks."

Instead of leaving, Michael proceeded to lower himself onto the comfy-looking storytelling chair, stretching his feet out before him.

Brittany pulled another button book from the bookshelf before absently running a hand across the aching small of her back. Most of the classroom furniture was geared to five-year-olds, and not to an adult woman five and a half feet tall. Consequently Brittany spent a lot of time bending over and by the end of a hard day her body sometimes complained about it.

Michael noticed her absent movement

and immediately voiced an offer. "Need a back rub?"

Brittany silently voiced her refusal with a quelling glance.

He returned her look with a phony look of innocence. "I was just asking."

Brittany made no reply. Instead she centered her attention on finishing the display for tomorrow's reading group. The books she'd chosen all dealt with buttons in one way or another. At one end of the table sat the button box, a metal cookie tin full of buttons of every imaginable color and size. She added a few button pictures the children had completed earlier in the year before stepping back to judge the overall effect.

The movement proved to be an unwise one on her part, for in stepping backward she tripped over Michael's outstretched ankles. Instinctively attempting to regain her balance, Brittany grabbed for the first thing at hand, which turned out to be the edge of the button box. The metal box flipped into the air, launching a hailstorm of buttons down around them.

Michael immediately jerked forward to break Brittany's fall. His firm grip on her waist was all that prevented her from ending up flat on her back on the floor. But having saved her, he then proceeded to take her from the frying pan into the fire by depositing her onto his lap. It all happened so fast that Brittany was momentarily stunned into speechlessness.

Michael's restraining fingers registered the expansion and contraction of Brittany's lungs as she fought to catch her breath. His fingers also registered the warmth of her skin beneath her cotton blouse. If he were to shift his hold slightly, the span of his fingers would come within touching distance of her firm breasts.

As if sensing his thoughts, Brittany grabbed his hands with her own. Her eyes flew to his with a mixture of outrage, disapproval, and confusion. If her first mistake had been not watching her step, her second error was looking into Michael's eyes at that moment. For his former inscrutability had been replaced with a heated hunger, and Brittany found herself caught up in the transformation.

The tiny flecks in his eyes conveyed but one message: *I want you; I want you, now.* The visual link was more compelling than any physical caress. No other man had ever looked at her in quite the same way, with an intensity that was tangible and a passion that was overwhelming. The combination wrought havoc on her nervous system, paralyzing her, hypnotizing her, luring her toward him.

"Have dinner with me," he said softly.

His words broke the bonds holding Brittany captive, freeing her voice as well as her will. She scrambled to her feet and stated her refusal most vehemently. "No way!"

CHAPTER THREE

Stung by her emphatic refusal, Michael responded with angry sarcasm. "Excuse me for asking!"

Brittany was well aware that she'd been more forceful than the circumstances had warranted. "I'm sorry, I didn't mean to be so blunt. But I thought I'd made my position clear."

Michael rose to his feet and glared at her. "That was before your position ended up being on my lap!"

Brittany glared right back. "That was an accident and it doesn't change the way I feel about dating my employees."

"So we're back to that, are we?" Michael unclenched his hands and jammed them into the back pockets of his jeans. "I am not an employee of this school." He said each word slowly and succinctly. "My paychecks are all marked with my company's logo and drawn from my company's bank account."

"I will not engage in an argument over semantics," Brittany retorted. "Regardless of the intimate details of your paycheck, the fact remains that you've been hired by this school and I am the director —"

"Interim director," he corrected her.

"— of this school. Interim or not."

"Okay, if you want to be strictly business-like, fine." Michael's eyes assumed a flinty remoteness. "Then tell me what you did to Bruno Maretti to make him quit."

"Bruno Maretti?" Brittany repeated.

"The massive, built-like-a-Sherman-tank security guard nicknamed Bruno the Bruiser, who's now selling shoes."

She nodded as recognition dawned. There'd been so many names. "I didn't know he was selling shoes."

"He is, thanks to you."

She frowned at the unfair accusation. "I didn't do anything."

"Come on, now. A man who's been work-ing in the security business for ten years up and quits after only one day on the job here. You must have done something." Michael challenged her silence by demanding, "Are you telling me you don't have any idea why he quit?"

"No, I'm not telling you that."

"So you do know what happened." Finally his interrogation was getting some-where.

"I know what happened, yes, but I can't tell you."

"Why not?"

"Because it would be betraying a confidence."

"Confidence!" This was getting ridiculous. "Whose confidence?"

"I promised Mr. Maretti that I wouldn't say anything." As far as Brittany was concerned that ended the matter.

Michael did not agree. "If one of my security guards did something wrong, so wrong that he was forced to swear you to secrecy before quitting, I want to know about it."

"Your security guard didn't do anything wrong," Brittany assured Michael. "He was merely a victim of circumstances."

"What circumstances?"

"That's all I have to say on the matter, Michael."

"I'm not one of your five-year-old students, Brittany. That tone of voice isn't going to work on me."

"At the risk of sounding repetitious, Michael, I don't need to use a certain tone of voice to work on you. *You* work for *me,* remember?"

Michael could feel himself losing his temper, which made him all the angrier. He shouldn't let her get to him, he'd dealt with difficult clients before. But something about this lady with the stylishly short hair and the glaring blue eyes reached out and grabbed him. And despite her attempts to deny it, he knew he'd had the same effect on her too.

"Now, if you'll excuse me, I've got other things to do aside from arguing with you."

After she'd made her regal exit, Michael could be heard to murmur, "Excuse you, Brittany Evans? As you said, 'No way!' "

Long after she'd left the school the impact of her encounter with Michael was still making itself felt, even during her dinner date with Richard Covington. Richard was an officer at Annapolis's famous Naval Academy and it was true, there was something striking about a man in uniform. Richard was in his mid-thirties, tall and lean. Actually Michael was just as tall, perhaps even an inch or two taller. . . .

Noting Brittany's spoon poised midair, Richard asked, "Is there something wrong with the soup?"

Brittany sent him a blank look before realizing her faux pas. She hurriedly lowered her spoon back to the bowl of tomato florentine soup. "No, there's nothing wrong. The soup's delicious," she assured him. Richard was still looking unconvinced so she hurriedly fabricated an explanation. "I was just thinking about something one of the kids said today."

"Really? What?"

For the second time in as many minutes, Brittany again sent Richard another blank look. "I beg your pardon?"

Richard patiently rephrased his question. "What did your student say?"

Brittany's mind went blank, but luckily her mouth was now full of soup, so she had some time to swallow and collect her thoughts. "I read the children a story about stone soup this afternoon. Daniel decided that dinosaurs must eat a lot of stone soup, that's what makes them so big."

Richard's polite smile made Brittany murmur self-consciously, "I guess you had to be there. . . . So, tell me about your day."

Her suggestion pleased him. Richard went on to talk about his work. Brittany tried valiantly, but she had a hard time following his words because her mind kept jumping back to Michael. The more she tried to wipe him from her thoughts, the more he was in them, and the angrier she became. The repetitious cycle prevented Brittany from enjoying her evening. Michael Devlin even invaded the privacy of her dreams that night, interrupting her sleep and leaving her with a lingering sense of restlessness.

The weather Tuesday morning reflected Brittany's mood. It was one of those rainy April days that poets claimed brought May flowers and everyone else claimed made them want to move to a drier climate. The weather was the least of Brittany's problems that morning, however.

To begin with, the slacks she'd planned on wearing turned out to be at the cleaners, so she had to find another outfit. By the time she'd teamed a pair of black jeans with a blue and black sweater with a geometric design she was already running late. Then, when Brittany opened her refrigerator door she discovered that the last of the orange juice was gone. To top it all off, while she was driving to work, the loose windshield wiper on her car flew off.

As far as Brittany was concerned, the entire series of mishaps were attributable to Michael Devlin. If he hadn't shaken her concentration yesterday, she would have remembered to take care of the things on the list in her purse; the list that said GO TO CLEANERS, PICK UP JUICE & YOGURT, STOP AT GARAGE FOR NEW WIPER. She always made lists. She rarely forgot them.

At least the rain would be good for one thing, Brittany decided as she dashed from her car to the school. Puddle Play. There was nothing like mucking around in the rain and jumping into puddles to get rid of one's frustrations. The children were thrilled with the idea; this was the first rainy day they'd had in a long time that was warm enough to make going outside feasible.

Joan and Marcia helped Brittany bundle the excited children into their rain gear.

Those who didn't have suitable rubber boots or rain slickers were given extras from the closet, where a jumble of raincoats, boots, and umbrellas were stored for just such an occasion as this.

Michael watched in silent astonishment as the line of umbrella-toting youngsters trouped past him, obviously on their way outside. Had the kids mutinied? But no, Marcia and Joan were similarly dressed. And there, at the end of the group, was Brittany, looking ridiculously cute in a navy-blue slicker and knee-high navy-blue rubber boots.

"Where are you going?" Michael demanded.

Brittany's reply was brief. "Outside."

"To play in the puddles," Daniel added, obviously excited at the prospect.

"But no kicking," Maria reminded him. In her arms was her ever-present doll, ingeniously wrapped in plastic to protect it from the inclement weather.

"I only kick when I'm a dinosaur," Daniel retorted. "Dinosaurs have to kick the water out of puddles. That's the way they're made."

"Then we'll just have to make sure you don't become a dinosaur until you're back inside the school, right, Daniel?" The tone of Brittany's voice made it clear that she'd better be right.

"Right, Msss Evans," Daniel agreed, using his unique blend of Miss and Ms.

"Besides, Daniel, dinosaurs are so unromantic." This observation, of course, came from Tiffany, whose avant-garde polka-dotted and striped multicolor raincoat made her stand out in the crowd of kindergartners. "You should be a frog, then you could be a prince in disguise."

"Frogs give people warts," Daniel stated.

"So can dinosaurs!" Tiffany returned.

"I hope you're not planning on going anywhere without protection." Michael directed his comment to Brittany.

"I wouldn't dream of it," she replied in a sweet little voice that should have warned him. "Which is why I brought this along." She gingerly held out a khaki-green rain poncho and let it drift over his desk. "For you. As are these." She dropped an old pair of thigh-high fishing boots on top of the poncho. "As soon as you put them on we'll proceed outside."

"Lady, you're crazy," Michael muttered under his breath so only she could hear. "It's pouring outside. Have you taken leave of your senses?"

Her senses were all present and vibrantly aware of the anger shooting from his green eyes. "I'm well aware of the weather, Mr. Devlin. That's precisely why we are going outside. To study the rain. Are you coming?"

"You don't give me much choice."

"Exactly." She turned away as he jerked the poncho over his head.

Michael followed her, his face set in an expression even more foreboding than the weather. His voice reflected his mood. "Now what?" he asked as they stood outside.

"We're only going around the school yard, Mr. Devlin," Brittany retorted. "Not to China."

Kevin piped up with, "I'd like to go to China."

"Me too," Adam agreed.

"Do they have dinosaurs in China?" Daniel asked.

"I think they have dragons," Adam told him.

"Dragons! Neato!" Daniel's eyes opened wide and his umbrella waved enthusiastically. "Can we go to China, Msss Evans?"

"Not today, Daniel," Brittany replied.

As they walked around the school grounds Michael listened to Brittany's soft voice talking to the children about the way rain helps things grow. He could see how good she was with kids. A real natural. Which sort of surprised him. Considering her bossy streak, he'd have expected her to rule with an iron fist rather than keep order with a soothing voice.

The mini-hike ended at the center of the playground where Brittany brought the children's attention to the various puddles dotting the ground and added a warning about wild splashing or kicking.

"What d'ya think's under here?" Kevin pondered as he gazed down at his own rain-spattered reflection and that of several of his classmates.

"Water," Matthew replied.

Kevin impatiently waved that answer aside. "I mean under the water."

"A fairy kingdom," suggested Carrie, who didn't speak often but when she did, it was with an imagination that matched Daniel's.

"Dirt," stated Matthew, ever the prosaic one.

"A television camera," claimed Tiffany.

"Do you think a television camera would fit under a puddle?" Brittany asked Tiffany. Her intention wasn't to dissuade Tiffany from her story, but rather to expand Tiffany's line of thought.

Sure enough, Tiffany did pause to seriously consider Brittany's question before saying, "It would fit but it might not work in the wet."

"Unless it was a magic camera run by fairies." Carrie thereby combined her ideas with Tiffany's to form a new story.

Adam stuck his hand in the middle of the puddle. "I don't feel any cameras. No fairies either."

"You can't feel fairies," Carrie explained.

"They're invisible."

No one could argue with that.

The hour chime on Brittany's alarm watch went off, signaling that Puddle Play time was over. The children were all guided back into the school, lured by the promise of hot cocoa in the kitchen.

"See, that wasn't so bad, was it?" Brittany inquired of Michael. She took his noncommittal grunt as agreement. "Good, because right after you drink your cocoa you'll be going out with Shelly and her class."

Intent on retribution for the way Brittany had dumped the rain gear and orders on him, Michael retorted, "Going out with Shelly is something I look forward to."

Brittany watched Michael and Shelly from her classroom window; watched them share an umbrella, laughing together, walking together. To her jaundiced eyes it appeared that Michael and Shelly were doing as much playing as the children were.

"Look, Ms. Evans!" Tiffany exclaimed. "I finished my rain picture." She waved the artwork in front of Brittany's face with unusual exuberance.

Brittany tore her gaze away from the window and said, "That's lovely, Tiffany. Are these two of your classmates?" She pointed to the stick figures standing close together.

"No, that's you and Mr. Devlin."

Now that she took a closer look, Brittany

saw that the two figures were apparently embracing. With all the surrounding splashes of yellow and purple rain, it was hard to notice at first glance, but there was no doubt that it was an embrace.

"I call it 'Romance in the Rain,'" Tiffany announced with a dramatic sigh. "What do you think?"

"I think it's sappy," Kevin announced before holding his own picture up for Brittany's perusal. "Mine's better."

Tiffany glared at Kevin. "It is not. Tell him, Ms. Evans."

"Kevin, everyone paints in a different way. That doesn't mean one painting is any better than another. Your painting is very good, so is Tiffany's."

But Kevin refused to be placated. "Painting is sissy stuff anyway."

"That's not true, Kevin. A lot of famous painters are men."

"Yeah? Name one."

"Michelangelo."

"Never heard of him."

And so it went. Brittany's day did not improve with time. In fact the next two days went equally badly as Michael and Shelly progressed from flirting to downright fawning. Brittany held on to her patience as long as she could before calling Shelly into her office Friday afternoon.

"Something wrong?" Shelly inquired, as if

she didn't already know the answer to that one. Brittany was not in the habit of calling her into the office during class unless there was a good reason.

"Yes, Shelly, something is wrong." Brittany's voice was brisk. "I won't beat around the bush with you. I'm unhappy with the way you've been reacting to Michael Devlin."

"Unhappy?" Shelly carefully flipped her long pale blond hair back over her shoulder. "Why?"

"Because I don't feel that it's very professional to discuss personal issues during working hours." When Shelly made no reply, Brittany asked, "Do you understand what I'm saying?"

Shelly nodded. "You don't want me fraternizing with Michael during working hours, is that it?"

"That's it."

"Why does my fraternizing with Michael bother you? You aren't interested in him yourself, are you?" Shelly looked at Brittany as if the idea just occurred to her.

"No, I'm not interested in him myself," Brittany denied angrily.

Shelly looked relieved at the news. "Good. Then what's the problem?"

"There's no problem as long as you fraternize after school hours and don't indulge in it here."

"Whatever you say. Is that all?"

"Yes, that's all."

"Okay."

Shelly left amid an awkward silence that always followed a dressing-down from the boss. She met Michael out in the hallway.

"Trouble?" he asked with a nod toward the closed door to Brittany's office.

Shelly nodded. "I've been officially notified that I'm to cease and desist fraternizing with you during working hours."

"You're kidding me!"

"I'm not."

A remarkably satisfied smile lifted Michael's lips. "Brittany actually said that, huh?"

"Not in those exact words. She was a bit more blunt."

"She was?" His smile widened.

"I don't understand what you're looking so pleased about," Shelly shot back, a bit miffed by his attitude. "Britt's not exactly happy with you either."

"What makes you say that?"

Now it was Shelly's turn to be oblique. "Call it feminine intuition."

Despite the fact that it was a Friday and he had work waiting for him at his office, Michael stayed late to talk to Brittany privately in her office.

"It got to you, didn't it?" he stated without preamble.

Brittany looked up from the class immunization records she was compiling. "What are you talking about?"

"The flirting with Shelly." He turned the office's single straight-backed chair backward before straddling it and resting his folded arms on the back. "It really got to you, didn't it?" There was no way that complacent statement was a question.

Brittany maintained her cool; it was tough but she managed. "If by 'got to you' you mean that it disturbed me, then the answer is yes. I'm disturbed when my employees allow their personal lives to interfere with their work."

"Bull!"

Her startled gaze bumped into his challenging stare. "I beg your pardon."

"You heard me. The reason you were disturbed had nothing to do with work."

"Really." She laid her pen on her desk and drawled, "How fascinating. I had no idea you'd taken up psychoanalysis. Do go on, Dr. Devlin."

"It's simple. You're jealous."

"You're crazy!"

"You're jealous," he repeated, pleased by her zealous retort.

"I am not!"

"You are too!"

"This is ridiculous," Brittany retorted. "I'm not going to sit here and argue with you the way Maria and Kevin would."

Michael nodded his approval. "Good, I'm glad to hear that." His voice lowered to a seductive pitch as he added, "And I'm glad that you stood up for yourself and warned Shelly off."

"I did not warn Shelly off."

"No? What would you call it?"

"I gave her a warning, certainly. The same one I'll give you. This is a school, not a playground for adults. If you want to go out with Shelly, fine. You can flirt with her and fawn over her as much as you like — so long as it's after hours and not here at work. Is that clear?"

"Crystal clear, Brittany. There's only one problem. I don't want to go out with Shelly. I want to go out with you."

"I've already told you —"

"I know what you've told me. I also know that it's an excuse." He rose from the chair with lazy grace and sauntered over to her desk, where he placed his hands palm-down on her blotter. Leaning forward, he softly warned her, "I'm not going to be your employee here at the school forever, Brittany. Sooner or later, you're not going to have that excuse to hide behind. What are you going to do then?"

Good question, Brittany. What are you going to do then?

CHAPTER FOUR

Michael arrived at his office half an hour later, and was enthusiastically greeted by his secretary, Arlene. "Long time no see! Cute T-shirt."

Michael looked down at the Percival School shirt, with its white lettering and logo of smiling sticklike figures, which he was still wearing. "Very funny. Any important messages?"

Arlene followed him into his office. "Let's see . . ." She consulted her notepad. "Aside from that pile of messages on your desk, there were two calls from your accountant this afternoon reminding you to sign your income-tax forms and return them to him by Monday morning, or else. Ray said to tell you that he landed the Ardmore Manufacturing account. Oh, and your brother-in-law called to remind you about your sister's surprise birthday party on Sunday."

"Damn!" Michael looked up from the sheets of correspondence Arlene had just handed him. "I forgot all about her birthday."

"Not surprising, considering all the extra

work you've been doing lately, holding down two jobs."

Michael jotted down a few gift ideas for his sister before saying, "The work at the school isn't that difficult."

Arlene wasn't swayed by his abstracted dismissal. "Then why are you doing it?"

"It's a challenge."

"Watching over thirty kids is a challenge? Or the school's director is a challenge?"

"Brittany is the interim director," Michael corrected her. "And since when do you ask your boss personal questions?"

"Since I first started working here," Arlene retorted, unafraid of Michael's pseudo-disapproval. "If Brittany Evans is this challenging, maybe you should ask her out."

"The idea has crossed my mind," Michael admitted with wry humor. "There's one major problem, though. She doesn't date her employees."

Arlene didn't understand the connection. "So? What's that got to do with you?"

Michael impatiently paced across the carpeted expanse of his office. "As long as I'm working at the school, Brittany considers me to be an employee."

"You're kidding!" One look at Michael's unamused face made Arlene hastily add, "You're not kidding." She shook her head in amazement. "This is even more complicated than I thought."

"Aren't you sorry you asked?"

"No."

"Well, I am. So let's get back to work." Michael proceeded to dictate half a dozen letters in reply to the correspondence Arlene had handed him earlier.

When he finally stopped dictating Arlene groaned and muttered, "Next time just stick bamboo shoots under my nails as punishment for my nosiness, but don't dictate at two hundred words a minute."

Arlene's words failed to register with Michael. Even here, surrounded by the familiar chaos of his desk, he was still preoccupied with Brittany. She infuriated him — at times he wondered what he saw in her. She intrigued him — most of the time he fantasized about the sexy woman beneath the bossy facade. She inflamed him — at all times he ached to have her.

As for Brittany, who knew what she was thinking? Once or twice he'd caught her looking at him with more than casual awareness, but she had generally been playing it cool. Until today, when she'd warned Shelly to stay away from him. Despite Brittany's denial, Michael was sure jealousy had motivated her. All he had to do was wait; Brittany wouldn't be able to fight him and herself for very long.

As Michael's second week at the school progressed, his optimistic prophecy proved to be correct, although Brittany went to great lengths to hide it. She was becoming more and more aware of him every day, every hour. She caught herself watching him at odd moments during the day. Instead of becoming accustomed to Michael, she was finding him to be increasingly charismatic.

Case in point were his eyes. They were green. So what? So she had gone beyond merely noticing their color; now she was reading his visual expressions, anticipating his mood by watching his eyes lighten with laughter or darken with need. She was noticing details like the shape of his eyebrows and the unexpected thickness of his eyelashes. Even the shape of his eyes had drawn her attention. His left eye slanted downward more than his right eye did.

This was getting ridiculous. But she couldn't stop. What was the matter with her?

Brittany was also increasing her understanding of Michael's body language. For instance she knew that he jammed his hands into his pockets when he was angry with her; that he tilted his head when he was amused. Arms folded across his muscular chest meant he was practicing patience. He rarely used a chair the way it was meant to be used, continually reversing it away from the table and swinging his leg over the seat. On those rare occasions when he did sit normally invariably his long legs were stretched out and crossed at the ankles.

Such preoccupation with Michael Devlin worried her. What had happened to her objectivity? It had obviously flown the proverbial coop.

She'd even started spending more time deliberating over what to wear to work each morning. Her job had always been hard on her clothing; her active pursuits with the children made pants her usual attire. But even normally tough jeans and slacks had a short life with her; if they didn't get splattered with paint or clay they ended up getting worn out at the knees owing to the amount of time she spent crouching down to her students' level. Recently, however, she'd had the wildest urge to put on that slinky dress she had stashed in her closet, or that off-white silk suit that had cost so much and looked so good.

So far she'd defied such temptation; neither outfit would last fifteen minutes in the kids' company without being devastated. Today she'd compromised, blending fashion with practicality by wearing her most flattering pair of slacks, dark turquoise corduroy stretch jeans. The collar of her purple polo shirt peeked out from beneath a stylish well-fitted short-sleeve sweatshirt.

The subtle upgrading of Brittany's wardrobe did not go unnoticed by Michael. He recognized the inroads he'd made in her defenses and eagerly anticipated even greater victories. In the interim his behavior toward Shelly was exemplary, pleasant but strictly professional. For her part, Shelly had all but given up on him.

Maria was the only one aside from Brittany who still eyed Michael with a degree of wariness. It took something as monumental as a broken doll carriage to sway Maria from her caution.

"Clarissa's grounded." Tiffany made the announcement to Brittany at precisely 10 A.M.

Clarissa was Maria's ever-present doll.

"What happened?" Brittany asked.

"The baby carriage is broken."

Brittany hurried over to the doll corner, where she found Maria forlornly holding up the bent wheel that had fallen off the carriage. "Can you fix it?"

Brittany tried, but the wheel refused to fit back into place. "Why don't you just carry Clarissa around until we can get the carriage fixed?"

Maria refused that suggestion with the obstinacy only a four-year-old can display. "No!"

Tiffany got an idea and hopped from one foot to the other as she verbalized it. "Ask

Mr. Devlin. I'll bet he knows how to fix it."

Hearing the commotion, Kevin came over to investigate. He waved away Tiffany's suggestion. "Aw, Maria won't go near Mr. Devlin. She's too scared."

"I am not!" Maria shouted.

Before Brittany could stop her, Maria had grabbed the mangled wheel and run out of the classroom with it.

The sound of Brittany's classroom door bursting open immediately caught Michael's attention. He watched in amusement as the formerly reticent and usually wary Maria stomped over to him and plunked down on his desk a wheel, obviously the worse for wear. "Fix it." She drew in a deep breath before adding an adorable smile and a sweet "Please."

"I see she's learning to practice her feminine wiles at an early age." Michael's words were directed to Brittany, who had followed Maria out into the front foyer.

Not understanding the relevance of Michael's comment, Maria frowned at him. "Can't you fix it?"

He directed his attention back to the little girl standing before him. "This wheel goes on something, right?"

Maria nodded. "My doll's baby carriage."

"If someone will bring me the carriage and a toolbox, I'll see if I can put it back on."

With the help of a hammer and a screwdriver, it took Michael less than ten minutes to reunite wheel and carriage. "There, it's as good as new." He gave the toy a test push to prove his point.

Maria beamed at him and took over as carriage pusher.

"Aren't you forgetting something?" Brittany gently reminded her.

Maria shook her head.

"How about thanking Mr. Devlin?" Brittany prompted.

"Oh. Thanks." Maria abandoned the carriage to walk over to Michael, tug him down to her level, and solemnly plant a smacking kiss on his cheek. "I like you now."

Brittany was surprised to see a hint of color wash over Michael's face. The moment she thought she had him pigeonholed, he showed some new side of himself that caused her to revise her estimation of him yet again. Did strong, silent types blush? Apparently this one did. Under certain circumstances.

As these thoughts were running through Brittany's mind, Maria guided the carriage back into the classroom.

"Cute kid," Michael said in a rough voice.

"That she is," Brittany agreed. She cleared her throat of the nervousness she suddenly felt. "Umm, while I'm out here, there is something I wanted to tell you. We'll be going on another outing this Thursday, weather permitting."

"What kind of weather?" Michael asked suspiciously, remembering the last little excursion he'd been on. The boots had leaked, and it had taken him the rest of the day to dry out his socks.

"No rain," she reassured him before adding, "We need a good wind, though."

"Wind? Why wind?"

"Because we're going to the park to fly kites."

"Why are *we* doing that?"

"It's all part of the learning experience," she explained.

"Whose learning experience? Yours or mine?"

Michael seemed to derive pleasure from shaking her composure. In the past two days his strategy had involved a sexual subtlety she'd never expected from him — a gentle touch, a burning look; never blatant but always effective. So effective that her pulse reacted to him like a metal detector to a silver mine.

Brittany fought the feeling and willed her heart rate back to normal. Thankfully her voice followed suit, displaying none of the breathlessness she felt. "I was referring to the children's learning experience. We use kite flying as a means of teaching them about wind and air currents."

Her explanation sounded like a lot of hot

air to Michael, but he wisely kept his views to himself.

The weather Thursday fulfilled all the requirements for kite flying. Brittany hadn't told the children about the excursion beforehand, in case the trip would have to be postponed. They greeted her news with cheers and whoops.

"Can I bring Clarissa?" Maria asked, holding up her doll.

"Sure you can," Brittany answered.

"Is Mr. Devlin coming too?" Maria inquired.

"Yes."

"Good. Clarissa likes him," she informed Brittany. "That's 'cause he fixed her carriage," she added, lest Brittany forget.

"I'm glad Clarissa likes Mr. Devlin," Brittany dutifully replied.

"Maria's got a crush on him," Kevin taunted.

"I do not," Maria immediately denied.

"Do too."

"Do not!"

Daniel interrupted their debate to ask, "Can I carry a kite? If I promise not to be a dinosaur?"

"No, let me!" Fifteen hands shot up in the air.

Brittany had to wait for the din to abate before she could be heard. "Mrs. Winston, Mrs. Shelding, and I will each carry a kite

73

to make sure they don't blow away before we get to the park."

The children accepted that explanation with varying degrees of graciousness.

"We've only got three kites," Adam complained. "There's more than three of us."

"That's right," Brittany agreed. "There are fifteen children and only three kites. What does that mean?"

"That we need to buy more kites," Matthew answered.

"Or we could wish for more kites, and maybe a passing fairy will hear us," Carrie suggested.

"What if we can't get any more kites?" Brittany asked the children. "Then what?"

"We have to share." The answer came from Maria.

"That's right."

Maria grinned at having supplied the correct answer.

Tiffany, however, looked aghast. "I don't like sharing," she exclaimed. "My mother shared her boyfriend once and she never got him back!"

"Sharing a kite is different," Brittany hastily assured Tiffany. Years of training had enabled Brittany to curb her reaction to whatever comments her students might come up with, but Tiffany occasionally managed to surpass even Brittany's wildest expectations. "We'll break into groups of five, like we do here in class for reading and art," she went on to explain in a soothing voice. "That way everyone in the group will get a chance to fly a kite."

"Then it might work," Tiffany allowed. "But it won't work with boyfriends."

"I'll keep that in mind, Tiffany," Brittany promised.

Since Shelly's morning class was also going kite flying in the park, the school would temporarily be empty. After making sure every student was outside and accounted for, Brittany activated the school's alarm system before locking the front door.

The park was only two blocks away. The caravan of children, thirty in all, wound its way down the sidewalk. Like the animals heading for Noah's Ark, they walked two-by-two, and sometimes three-by-three if they could get away with it. Interspersed at strategic points throughout the group were the four teacher's assistants as well as Brittany, Shelly, and Michael.

As the children walked, Brittany and Shelly took turns pointing out the surrounding signs of spring. A robin's nest spotted in a tree was worth stopping for. So was a budding hedge fronting a historic house dating back to the eighteenth century.

Once they'd reached the park, Michael was of the opinion that getting there was half the fun. He'd stationed himself near the back of the group so he could keep an eye on the children for security purposes. His position also allowed him to keep an eye on Brittany, who was decked out in tight jeans and a Percival School T-shirt. Actually, all the school's employees were wearing jeans and the official T-shirt, but somehow the uniform looked particularly appealing on Brittany.

Michael's eyes turned to Shelly, then back to Brittany. Two women; both attractive. Why did one leave him cold and the other hot with excitement? Why did one barely strike his fancy while the other ignited his passion without even trying? Whatever the reason, he intended having Brittany Evans, and having her soon.

While Michael was plotting his intimate and ultimate game plan, Shelly and Brittany were directing the children into groups of five. Each group had a supervising adult who then took charge of preparing the group's kite for flight. The primary assignment was completing the kite's tail.

Brittany and her five charges all sat on a picnic bench while the kite and a square of thin cotton lay on the tabletop before them. "Now before our kite will fly we need to put a tail on it," Brittany said.

"Why?" Maria asked.

"The kite needs a tail to balance it so it will fly better."

"A tail like a horse?" Carrie asked.

"Horses don't fly," Matthew told Carrie.

"They do if they're magic horses," Carrie retorted.

"There's no such thing as magic horses," Matthew dismissed.

"What do you know?" Maria countered belligerently. "You don't even believe in the tooth fairy!"

Brittany sidetracked Matthew by having him help her rip the cotton into strips. The other children followed his example and ripped the material — sometimes incorrectly, but always with enthusiasm. Those who knew how to tie knots were able to utilize their skill by tying the strips together to form a tail.

"Can you think of anything else that has a tail?" Brittany asked those whose skills did not yet include knot tying.

"A cat."

"A dog."

"Daniel's pictures of dinosaurs."

"You're all right," Brittany congratulated them with a laugh.

From his central position Michael was able to keep tabs on all six groups, although his attention did stray to Brittany a bit more often than to the others. Through squinted eyes he watched the way the sunlight bounced off her hair, sparking it with copper and gold. He couldn't hear what she was telling the children but he could see the enthusiasm with which she said it. Her face was animated, her lips parted with laughter.

Reluctantly, Michael tore his attention away from Brittany to check on the status of the other groups. Regardless of his feelings for her, Michael had a job to do and was always vigilant for trouble. And trouble was what Joan Shelding was having getting her group's kite into the air.

When Michael offered his assistance, Joan gratefully accepted. "I'm a whiz with mechanical things," she said, "but kite flying is not my strong point."

"Is this a man's job?" Tiffany asked Michael.

"Not really," he answered. "Brittany — I mean Ms. Evans — seems to have gotten her kite up in the air without any trouble." Michael pointed to Brittany, who was joyfully tugging on the roll of string anchoring her group's soaring kite to the earth.

Tiffany nodded. "Yeah, but Ms. Evans can do anything. She's a teacher."

Michael didn't know what to say to that so he concentrated on unknotting the kite's lopsided tail. "There, now it should fly fine."

"Let me try, let me try!" Adam requested.

Michael looked to Joan for approval before

handing the kite to Adam. "Here, hold it like this with your right hand," he instructed the youngster. "Higher. Okay, now run into the wind, this way." Michael aimed Adam in the right direction, but Adam was too short to make the most of the favorable breeze. The kite fluttered out behind Adam as long as he kept running, but as soon as he stopped, the kite dropped to the ground like a rock.

"Something's wrong," Tiffany observed solemnly.

"This kite stinks!" Adam declared.

Michael rescued the kite from Adam's disgusted hands before any damage could be done to the fragile wood and paper construction.

"Don't give up yet. Let me try." However, when Daniel's attempt had the same results, he said, "You're right, Adam. This kite's busted."

"Let Mr. Devlin try," Tiffany suggested. "He's taller so he's already closer to the sky."

Michael held the kite with a competence drawn from years of kite-flying experience. Granted his last experience was a good fifteen years ago, but surely kite flying was like bike riding, a skill you never lost. Keeping that thought in mind, Michael began running into the wind, his gaze fixed on the bright blue and yellow kite hovering past his right shoulder. He let out some string and watched the distance between himself and the kite grow.

Smelling success, Daniel and Adam ran after Michael, shouting words of encouragement.

Brittany paused in her explanation of the aerodynamics of kite flying to watch Michael running. He moved like a well-oiled machine, only no machine could ever look this good! Michael's physical ability was apparent in the smooth coordination of his strides.

Even as she was appreciating the piston-like motion of his powerful legs, Michael stumbled over something and went sprawling facedown on the grass. Daniel and Adam, running behind him, didn't have time to stop. They toppled on top of Michael in a unique adaptation of a classic football tackle.

Brittany arrived at the scene seconds later, followed by a majority of the kids. Joan was already helping Daniel and Adam to their feet. They were slightly shaken up but unhurt, their fall having been broken by Michael's body. Michael, however, still lay on the ground, not moving.

As Shelly herded most of the children away, Brittany dropped to Michael's side, her fingers automatically searching for a pulse along his neck. She found it, throbbing beneath her fingertips. His skin was warm and slightly rough. Her index finger strayed inadvertently and brushed against his jaw, where the roughness of an impending beard awakened all the nerve endings in her fleshy fingertip. A ripple of sensual delight slid up her arm and spread throughout her body.

This is no time for cheap thrills, Brittany, she reprimanded herself. *The man could still be hurt.*

Her voice was shaky as she asked, "Michael, are you all right?"

There was no answer. Not a good sign.

Brittany repeated her question, this time lowering her lips to Michael's ear. Her hand, which was still lightly braced upon his back, felt his deep inhalation as Michael dragged air into his oxygen-starved lungs. With a groan he gingerly rolled onto his back.

"Is he dead?" Daniel asked in a hushed voice.

"He can't groan if he's dead," Matthew pointed out.

"But his eyes are closed," Adam said.

"And he doesn't look so good," Kevin added.

"He needs the kiss of life," Tiffany exclaimed dramatically. "Ms. Evans, you have to give him the kiss of life! You know, artificial insemination!"

"It's called artificial *respiration,* Tiffany, and I don't think it's necessary. Mr. Devlin will be fine. He's just had the wind knocked out of him." Although after Tiffany's last misnomer, Brittany felt as if she were the one gasping for breath.

Tiffany, however, was not about to give up on her idea. "If the wind was knocked out, then you should knock it back into him by kissing him," she stated.

Brittany's hand, which had been resting on Michael's back before he'd turned around, now rested on his chest and monitored the increasing steadiness of his breathing. However, his eyes were still shut and he showed no sign of having heard Tiffany's verbal mix-up. Brittany was sure that if Michael had heard it, he would be making the most of it somehow, and his inertness worried her. Her hand shifted so that she could monitor the rate of his heartbeat, which seemed unusually fast. Perhaps he'd cracked a rib when he'd fallen.

"How come you're lookin' under his shirt?" Daniel asked Brittany.

"Maybe she's gonna kiss him better," Maria said.

"You have to kiss him on the lips," Tiffany advised Brittany. "Otherwise it won't work."

"On the lips? Yuck! That's gross!" Kevin declared.

Brittany ignored the debate raging around

her and ran her fingers over Michael's ribs, trying to ascertain if any bones were protruding where they shouldn't. There were no open wounds.

"That . . . tickles," Michael muttered in an unsteady undertone, finally opening his eyes.

"Are you all right?" Brittany asked for the third time.

"Sure, I'm fine." He cautiously moved his legs and arms as if testing to make sure they were all still attached.

Once she saw Michael was okay, Tiffany spoke again. "Aren't you going to kiss him, Ms. Evans?"

"No."

Tiffany's face fell. Her "Oh" was thick with disappointment.

"He doesn't need me to kiss him," Brittany felt impelled to explain.

"Sure I do," Michael murmured.

Still leaning over him, Brittany turned her head to deliver a reprimand. Michael, however, had other ideas. He lifted his head and brought his lips to hers. Had the kiss stopped there, the situation could have been dismissed lightly. But the kiss did not stop there.

Michael's hand moved up from his side to cup the back of her head, his fingers sinking into the surprising softness of her hair. He drew her more deeply into his embrace, exploiting the fact that Brittany's lips had already been parted to express her disapproval. His mouth was warm and moist. There were no attacking tongue-thrusts, only tempting circular motions and the slightest of nibbles.

Brittany's eyes closed with pleasure. The ripple of sensual delight she'd experienced at the simple action of brushing her finger against his face was magnified tenfold as excitement rushed through her body. She was enticed into desiring his kiss — desiring and returning it.

Tasting her response, Michael threw caution to the wind. Her hand, which lay resting on his chest, felt his hungry groan before he tugged her closer to him. Her supporting arm collapsed, tumbling her onto his chest. Luckily there were only a few inches separating them so Brittany's fall did not again knock the wind out of him.

Instead she knocked all thought clear out of his mind. The feel of her soft breasts pressed against his chest sent his heartbeat into overdrive. The feel of his arising passion sent Brittany into a panic as she abruptly imagined the circle of childish faces looking down on them.

Even as Brittany was breaking away from Michael, Tiffany was stating her views. "Now, that's romantic!"

"*That's* how my teenage cousin Anna got into trouble," Adam retorted.

Brittany knew the feeling. There was no doubt about it. Michael Devlin spelled trouble with a capital T!

CHAPTER FIVE

The next day Brittany's troubles were compounded by the imminent arrival of Percival School's annual Spring Festival. The festival would take place that weekend and there was still a lot of work that had to be done by tomorrow. She welcomed the distraction the preparations provided because it helped her block out yesterday's interlude with Michael.

Unfortunately the treatment was not one hundred percent effective. Brittany's Friday class schedule included a kitchen project, which meant that she was closer to Michael's security station than she cared to be. He sat right outside the door, his chair positioned so that he could see into the kitchen as well as keep tabs on the main entrance and Shelly's classroom.

Brittany was very much aware of Michael's eyes on her, following her as she moved around the kitchen. Today they were making no-cook coconut pastel bonbons. The finished candies would proudly be offered to parents tomorrow at the festival. But first Brittany had to make sure the candies reached completion; it was no good counting their bonbons before they were hatched! Especially when Daniel was pilfering their supply of grated coconut.

"Daniel, we agreed not to taste any more of the ingredients, remember?"

"I know, Msss Evans, but dinosaurs really love coconut."

"Dinosaurs aren't allowed in the kitchen, Daniel. They aren't allowed to beat the cream cheese either." Brittany held up a plastic mixing spoon invitingly. "Are you sure you want to be a dinosaur right now?"

Daniel made his decision with split-second quickness. "I'll be a dinosaur later."

"Good." Brittany handed Daniel the spoon and a bowl of softened cream cheese and watched him concentrate his energy on beating.

Meanwhile Matthew had taken it upon himself to supervise the measuring of the confectioner's sugar, a job he was doing with scientific precision. "Add a little more," he instructed Carrie. But her idea of a little didn't coincide with Matthew's. "No!" he exclaimed in horror. "That's too much! It's way over the line now!"

"Just take some out, then," Carrie suggested, wiping her sugar-coated hands on her apron.

Eventually the two and a half cups of powdered sugar were measured to Matthew's approval and dumped into the now-blended cream cheese. Another energetic volunteer, Kevin this time, took over as chief blender, while Maria was allowed to pour in the quarter teaspoon of vanilla. When Adam and Tiffany generously began adding the food coloring, Brittany and Marcia barely saved the mixture from neon brightness instead of pastel lightness.

"Okay, now we refrigerate that for one hour," Brittany told the children.

"What are we gonna do while it's in there?" Adam asked, still holding the tiny food-coloring bottle clasped in his hand.

Brittany gently took the bottle away from him. "First thing we do is clean up in here." With Joan and Marcia's assistance, the children were organized into a work force that soon had the kitchen restored to order.

Brittany wished that her peace of mind were as easily restorable. Did Michael have to keep staring at her like that? She glanced at him over one shoulder. Insisting he wear jeans and a Percival School T-shirt may have been a mistake, she abruptly decided. Surely Michael wouldn't look as good in a regulation security guard uniform? After all, a uniform wouldn't mold his muscular chest as faithfully as a snug-fitting cotton T-shirt did, nor would it bring out the green of his eyes.

Those same green eyes were presently

freely roving over Brittany's curves. The earthy, masculine perusal went beneath the apron, beneath the crisp tan slacks and red tailored rayon shirt she wore. His gaze intimately peeled each layer of clothing away from her until, in his eyes, she was standing there wearing nothing but a blush. Reading his thoughts as clearly as if they were printed in boldfaced print, Brittany could practically feel the touch of his eyes on her skin, could feel the blood rushing through her body.

"You're turning all red, Ms. Evans," Carrie said. "Are you hot?"

"A little, Carrie," she admitted.

"I know how you feel, Ms. Evans," Michael offered from his position near the door. The gleam in his eyes told her he took full credit for her rise in temperature. "I'm rather warm myself."

"Perhaps you're catching the flu, Mr. Devlin," Brittany retorted as she passed his desk.

"Something's definitely bitten me, Ms. Evans," he murmured for her ears only. "I ache all over. . . ."

His voice was reaching out to her in a way that his arms, for the time being, couldn't.

"Now what do we do?" Daniel's demanding question interrupted them.

Michael let his eyes do the talking. They

spoke of the intimate things he'd like to do to her — now.

Brittany tore her gaze away with surprising difficulty. "Now we work on the display cabinet, Daniel."

"I like what I've seen you display so far, Ms. Evans," Michael murmured as she began to move away from him.

"You might not like a display of my temper," Brittany made it a point to toss back. "I wouldn't push my luck if I were you."

"You sound like my parents right before they're gonna have a big fight," Daniel told them in a complaining voice.

"We weren't fighting, Daniel," Brittany assured her student.

"That's right," Michael agreed. "I would never fight with Ms. Evans."

"Me either," Daniel said. "She's a teacher."

"I know." Michael directed an intimate smile in Brittany's direction. "But she still has a few things to learn."

Daniel was confused. "Teachers know everything."

Brittany shot Michael a "now-look-what-you've-done" look. "This teacher knows that we're running out of time," she briskly told Daniel. "If we want to finish the display we'd better get to work."

Joan had already opened the glass display case that was reserved for Brittany's class. The second glass case was for the afternoon class that Ann taught, while the third and fourth cases across the way had already been filled with projects from Shelly's morning and afternoon classes.

Marcia, meanwhile, had brought along the name-plates on which the children had previously printed their names. Each child had already picked his or her favorite project to put in the display case next to their names. The children were now eagerly awaiting the arrangement of their treasures.

"Put my butterfly in first," Tiffany demanded. The egg-carton butterfly she held in her hand was a recently completed craft project, and bore the stamp of Tiffany's unique personality. The construction-paper wings were done in two colors; the left wing was red, the right purple. Both were decorated with a splashy assortment of dots and squiggles. The butterfly's face was also eye-catching, the center point being its mouth, which had a huge pipe-cleaner tongue hanging out of it.

Brittany took Tiffany's selection and placed it in the case beside Tiffany's name-plate.

"Butterflies are sissy stuff," Kevin snorted. "Puppets are better." Not surprisingly, Kevin's contribution to the display was his paper-bag puppet on which he'd drawn the evil face of his favorite villain.

"Dinosaurs are the best," Daniel maintained as Brittany placed his clay dinosaur figure next to Kevin's paper-bag puppet.

"They are not." Matthew carefully handed Brittany his Styrofoam-ball rendition of an atom. "Atoms are even more interesting," he said.

"I am?" Adam asked.

"I said at-oms, not Adam," Matthew explained. "Atoms. You know. Science."

"Oh, right." Adam nodded as if he knew what Matthew was talking about. "I forgot." The excuse was Adam's favorite; he used it frequently.

"It looks like you're getting ready for something really special," Michael observed from his ringside seat at the security desk. "All this cooking and decorating. What's going on?"

"Tomorrow's our spring festi-something," Maria told Michael with the beaming smile she now reserved solely for him.

"Spring Festival," Matthew meticulously corrected Maria.

Maria nodded with excitement. "Yeah, and there's gonna be a show of all our pictures and our parents are coming and they're gonna bring neato food and we get to play games and . . . and . . . and I can't remember all the rest but there's lots more!"

The only item among the "lots more" that gave Brittany cause to worry was tomorrow's auction. A frown was already forming on her forehead as the children all tromped back into the kitchen to complete the final step of their bonbon-making. She stood by, watching the children shape the chilled dough into small balls and roll them around in the grated coconut, and thought about tomorrow.

Now that it was too late, Brittany was beginning to have second thoughts about her contribution to tomorrow's activities. The auction was the festival's largest money-maker, with parents of past and present students contributing most of the goods or services. Traditionally, a box lunch with the school's director was one of the items auctioned off each year and Brittany had agreed to fill in for Doris as item number nineteen on the as-yet-undisclosed auction list.

But ever since Michael had kissed her yesterday, he'd been looking at her as if he were a sultan and she his slave. Understandably that made her leary of her scheduled appearance tomorrow on the auction block! Of course, there was no indication that Michael would even be attending tomorrow's festivities. In fact, the more she thought about it, the more convinced she was that she ought to dissuade Michael from attending.

Brittany had her arguments all ready

when Michael spoke to her about the festival after school that afternoon.

He came into her office, sank into the chair across from her desk, stretched out his long legs, and crossed them at the ankles before speaking. "Sounds like tomorrow's going to be a big day."

Brittany eyed his legs with caution. She had no intention of accidentally tripping over his feet again, so she stayed safely seated in her office chair. "It's our Spring Festival, yes, but you won't be required to work tomorrow."

"That's good."

Brittany felt relief at his words. The feeling was short-lived.

"That means I'll be free to attend the festival on my own time," Michael went on to state with a satisfied grin.

"I'm sure you've got better things to do with your time," she said nonchalantly, knowing Michael well enough to realize that any protest on her part would only increase his desire to attend.

He deliberately twisted her words. "You don't consider this festival to be worthwhile?"

"Of course it's worthwhile. The festival helps fund some of our programs." She took a deep breath before continuing. "I merely meant that it's geared to the children and their parents. You'd probably be bored."

"I don't bore easily," he told her, eying her mouth with a predatory interest she found disconcerting.

As a last measure she warned him, "If you do come we will put you to work, manning one of the booths or something — even if it is your day off."

Michael was not dissuaded by her threat. "Fine. See you tomorrow, then."

Despite a relaxing dinner date with Richard, vivid dreams of a sultan and his harem still plagued Brittany's slumber that night. Richard had promised to show up at Saturday's festival and Brittany hoped that his appearance would help mitigate Michael's magnetic effect on her.

She dressed Saturday morning with a vigilance for protocol more suitable for a formal state dinner than a school spring festival. Two outfits were discarded as being too provocative; another for being downright boring. Finally she struck a happy medium between the two extremes. Her eventual choice was a cotton skirt and matching turquoise blouse that were designed to pass as a dress. Her accessories were all white, from the stylish clips in her freshly washed hair to the sheer stockings on her legs. Her shoes, however, were soft leather ballet-type slippers in a turquoise one shade darker than her blouse.

Brittany had always been a sucker for shoes; her crammed closet floor attested to that fact. She shut the louvered doors to her closet, watered her five-year-old avocado plant, picked up the soon-to-be-bidden-upon boxed lunch, and bravely walked out of her apartment, ready to face whatever trials might be ahead of her.

The weather was fully cooperating by providing a sunny day that was the very epitome of spring. Brittany spent the morning hours before the festival opened organizing the transformation of the school's playground into a fairground. Joan and Marcia were in charge of setting up the clothesline art show. A brightly colored nylon rope went from the swing set to the horizontal climbing ladder, and both women were busy fastening the children's paintings on the taut rope with white plastic clothespins.

In another corner volunteers were setting up the popular bake-sale table. Not far away was another popular attraction, the old-fashioned popcorn-making pushcart which belonged to a former student's restaurateur father. Colorful balloons were being inflated from a tank of helium by still more volunteers.

Things were going so smoothly that Brittany knew something had to go wrong. It did, in the shape of a phone call from the wife of their scheduled auctioneer. The poor man had developed a bad case of laryngitis and wouldn't be able to conduct the auction. Brittany was pondering over a possible replacement when inspiration struck in the form of Michael Devlin.

Brittany saw him the moment she returned to the playground. Michael was dressed in jeans, but a loose white shirt had replaced the green T-shirt he was required to wear when working. The shirt's short sleeves had been rolled up into a tight cuff, which clung to the powerfully developed muscles of his upper arm. A wide leather belt rested around his waist with well-worn familiarity. A gentle breeze billowed his shirt and gave Brittany the momentary impression of a swashbuckling corsair. The illusion was reinforced by the piratical smile he tossed her way.

Michael didn't say a word about the way she looked. No compliments about the color of her outfit or the style of her hair. There was no need. The way he looked at her said it all.

In that brief moment Brittany decided the safest place to put Michael was at the auctioneer's podium, where he wouldn't be able to bid on her!

"I've got a job for you," she told him.

When the auction got under way an hour later Brittany was amazed at the ease with which Michael rattled off the bids. *Was*

97

there such a thing as a smooth-talking strong and silent type? she wondered.

"Come on, folks, this slide rule is worth more than five dollars," Michael was telling the crowd. "You can use it as a wall decoration or even use it to train your dog."

"Six dollars," Daniel's father bid.

"Thank you, sir. Six dollars it is. Six-fifty anyone?" Michael held up the slide rule for everyone to see. "This is your last chance. No? Six dollars — once, six dollars — twice, sold for six dollars to the lucky man who knows a good bargain when he sees one."

The audience applauded in humorous appreciation.

And so Michael progressed from item number two — an hour with a tax accountant — through item number eighteen — a pair of tickets to a sold-out performance at Washington's Kennedy Center for the Performing Arts. By car the nation's capital was only forty minutes west of Annapolis, so the tickets were a hotly contested item.

Those tickets were also the last item before her box lunch. As Brittany made her way toward the podium, her stomach was clenched in a nervous knot, her eyes glued on Michael. He returned her stare with an inscrutable expression guaranteed to foil the best of cryptologists. With a talent like that, he was probably a pro at poker. Did he have something up his sleeve?

"We've saved the best for the last, ladies and gentlemen," Michael announced. "Item number nineteen is a two-hour picnic lunch with Percival School's interim director, the lovely Brittany Evans."

Having typed that list herself, Brittany knew that the adjective was Michael's addition. Hopefully that would be his only ad-lib remark.

Michael dashed her hopes by stating, "We'll open the bidding at thirty dollars."

Thirty! Brittany almost dropped the picnic basket she'd just placed on the bidding table. That was double the amount she'd listed as an opening bid.

Despite the higher sum, Daniel's parents, Carrie's parents, and Richard all entered into a bidding war. Michael repeated their offers. "Thirty-five, forty. Come on, she's worth more than that! Forty-five, good, forty-six, forty-seven, fifty." The last bid was Richard's. "Is that it, ladies and gentlemen? Fifty dollars? Fine." But before hitting the gavel to close the deal, Michael proceeded to enter into the bidding himself. "One hundred dollars."

The audience twittered in surprise, and speculation ran rampant.

"You're the auctioneer, you can't make a bid!" Brittany angrily informed him.

"I just did. One hundred dollars," Michael repeated, in case anyone hadn't heard him the first time.

Not to be outdone, Richard offered, "One hundred and twenty."

Michael coolly upped the ante. "Two hundred."

Richard shook his head to indicate that he was out of the running. "Sold for two hundred dollars." Michael banged the gavel and closed the auction.

Brittany was seething. "I can't believe you did that!"

Michael pulled a handful of wrinkled twenties from his wallet and handed them over to Joan, who was acting as record-keeper. He then took Brittany by the arm and started moving off with her. "Why not? Aren't you worth it?"

"I wasn't up for auction. All you bought was my boxed lunch. So where do you think you're dragging me?" she demanded, trying to free her elbow from his clasp.

"I'm not dragging you anywhere, yet. I'm simply hurrying you along to our picnic date."

Brittany immediately set him straight. "This is not a date and I can't leave now, the festival isn't over yet."

"Britt, where are you off to?" Richard questioned, having finally pushed through the crowd to catch up with her.

"Introduce us, Brittany," Michael instructed her.

"Richard Covington, Michael Devlin."

"You broke the rules, Mr. Devlin," Richard informed him.

Michael's smile was a warning. "I usually do."

Tiffany saved the day by running up to Michael and asking him, "You wanna meet my mother?"

"I'd really like to, Tiffany, but —"

"Good." Tiffany took Michael by the hand and dragged him off.

There was something rather touching about the brawny security guard being led away by the artful little girl. Compared to Tiffany's petiteness, Michael appeared to be a massive giant.

"Britt, what are you going to do about this picnic thing?" Richard was demanding.

Brittany switched her attention to Richard's disgruntled face. "I don't see what I can do, Richard. He's already made his donation."

"It wasn't legal. He was out of order."

"Yes, I know that." *Michael is always out of order,* she silently tacked on. "But it's water under the bridge now. The most expeditious way of dealing with the situation is to let him have the box lunch."

"Britt, the man didn't shell out two hundred bucks for a box lunch."

"That's all he's going to get," she retorted with vehement determination.

Michael came to reclaim her shortly thereafter. He ignored Richard completely and showed Brittany his watch. "It's already three in the afternoon. When did you plan on serving this picnic lunch of yours?"

Brittany decided that it would be better to get this over with now. The sooner she went with Michael, the sooner her two hours would be up. Besides, the festival was scheduled to last another three hours. If she left now she could still be back in time to help wrap things up.

"Let's go, we can eat at the park where we went kite flying," she decided. "I'll talk to you later, Richard," she promised the other man before Michael hauled her away.

"I see your tastes run to Ivy Leaguers," Michael muttered as he marched her away from the school and down the block.

"Richard is an officer at the Naval Academy," she proudly announced.

"Bully for him." Michael abruptly stopped their forward motion and veered over to the curb. "Here, put this on." The next thing she knew Michael was setting a huge helmet over her head. His fingers brushed against her skin as he fastened the safety straps under her chin. "Okay, now get on."

"Get on?"

"Yeah." Michael nodded at the massive

motorcycle parked at the curb. "Get on."

He slipped a helmet over his own head while Brittany just stood there, with picnic basket in hand, staring at him and the machine as if they'd landed from an alien planet. "You're joking, aren't you?"

"What's the problem?"

"The problem is that I'm not about to get on that thing." Brittany would have taken off the helmet, but she couldn't figure out how to undo the straps.

He looked at her with mocking skepticism. "Don't tell me you've never ridden on a bike before?"

"Not a bike like this," she retorted, eying the powerful machine. "Even if I had, I'm certainly not dressed for it now. And where would we put the picnic basket?"

"No problem, I'll take care of the basket." He took it from her and handed it over to a passing family obviously on their way from the school. "Glad you visited the Spring Festival, folks. You're the one hundredth visitor today, and to celebrate we've got this lovely picnic-basket lunch for you. Enjoy, enjoy." With a hearty pat on the man's back, a wink at the woman, and a grin for their five-year-old daughter, Michael sent them on their way.

He then turned back to Brittany. "Your skirt's no problem either. Look, I'll show you." Without further ado, Michael put his hands on her waist and lifted her onto the black leather seat as if he were setting her on a hobby horse. "There. Now put your feet here . . ." He guided her turquoise leather shoes onto a metal rod. "And put your arms around me," he instructed as he hopped onto the bike and switched on its engine.

Brittany had no choice but to put her arms around his waist and hold on to him for dear life. It was that or end up in a heap on the street!

"You're doing fine!" Michael shouted the words of encouragement to her over his shoulder as he turned a corner at what felt like sixty miles an hour. "See? There's nothing to it."

"I wouldn't know, my eyes are shut," she muttered against his back.

It was another two blocks before Brittany felt safe enough to peek through clenched eyelids. The first thing she saw were the red brick outer walls of the Naval Academy whizzing past her. Michael was on the road leading out of town.

"Where are you going?" she shouted in his ear.

"It's a surprise."

"I don't like surprises."

"You'll like this one."

Since throttling Michael was bound to affect his driving, Brittany discarded the idea, tempting though it may have been. Their mode of travel was hazardous enough as it was. She judiciously decided that she'd wait for a more opportune moment to end this highway abduction.

She thought her moment might have arrived when Michael pulled into a roadside seafood shanty. But he didn't get off the motorcycle. Instead he pulled up to the take-out window and ordered two hearty baskets of fried clams and some birch beer, the local equivalent of root beer.

"Why don't we eat here?" Brittany demanded over the rumble of the cycle.

"I've got a better place in mind," he told her.

There was little Brittany could do from her position on the back of the still-idling machine. *Besides,* she guiltily admitted, *the clams did smell delicious.* What the heck. Her situation wasn't serious enough to warrant making a huge scene, so she decided to wait and see what else Michael had up his sleeve.

After paying for their meal, Michael took the white paper bag containing their order and stowed it in a storage compartment on the bike. "The place I've got in mind isn't far away," he told her. "Hang on."

She did, and they were off again. A few miles later Michael turned off the paved road onto what felt like little more than a cow path. After a few minutes he brought the bike to a stop and cut the engine. Looking at the neighboring field of wildflowers, he decided, "This is a nice spot for a picnic. What do you think?"

"That you're crazy!"

Michael was not upset by her declaration. "End of the line," he announced. "This is where we get off."

Get off? He had to be kidding! She'd be lucky if she could still stand after that bone-jarring ride.

"On the other hand, if you want to sit here with your arms around me, I wouldn't mind that either." She could hear the amusement in his voice.

She pulled her arms from around his waist and held on to the backrest, of sorts, that she'd just discovered was behind her.

Michael smoothly dismounted from the bike and removed his helmet. He absently ruffled his fingers through his hair, a procedure that lent him the tousled look of a mischievous boy. But that body definitely belonged to a man!

Michael plucked her off the back of the cycle with the same ease he'd displayed in putting her on it. Despite her worries, Brittany discovered that her legs did support her. They felt a little wobbly, but at least they didn't collapse.

While she was regaining her land legs, so

to speak, Michael was retrieving their lunch and a blanket from the bike's storage compartment. Holding both items in one arm, he then took Brittany by the hand. "Come on. Watch where you step."

Too late. Brittany stepped into a mud puddle. "My shoes!"

"Here, you hold these." Michael shoved the blanket and paper bag into her arms and proceeded to whisk her up into his arms. He walked through the mud with a supreme indifference to his already well-worn leather boots.

Held against him as she was, Brittany could feel every step Michael took. His muscular arms cradled her protectively as he carried her. Her left arm was occupied with holding the blanket and food he'd handed her, but her right arm was free to coil around the back of his neck.

Michael's nearness brought about a host of sensual discoveries. She discovered that his brown hair was thick with an almost silky texture that was slightly incongruous with his tough-guy image. She discovered that the chest she was resting against was hard and warm beneath the soft cotton of his shirt, and that she could feel the supple play of his muscles with every step he took.

He walked almost to the center of the field before he set her down very carefully. "Stay right there until I lay this blanket out."

The fear of further damage to one of her favorite pairs of shoes ensured Brittany's obedience.

"There." Michael led her by the hand onto the invitingly soft blanket much as a doorman would help a lady into a cab. "Okay, now sit down and kick off your shoes."

Brittany frowned at his order. "What for?"

"Comfort. That's what I'm going to do."

Sure enough, Michael pulled off his boots before sinking down next to her. He then dug into their bag of food.

"Here, one for you and one for me." He handed her a paper basket full of the crisp fried clams.

Brittany devoured her helping with an unexpectedly hearty appetite. The seafood and the accompanying french fries tasted delicious, especially when washed down by the mellow carbonated taste of birch beer. She finished every last bit of her meal.

"You've got tartar sauce on your face," Michael said with deceptively casual interest.

"I do?" She dabbed at her cheek with a napkin. "Where?"

Leaning forward, Michael took the paper napkin away from her and said, "Right here." But instead of using the napkin, he brushed his lips across the corner of her mouth before his tongue darted out on its cleanup mission.

"This really isn't necessary," Brittany murmured in a strangled voice.

Michael's contradiction was huskily voiced. "Yes, it is." He added another swirl of his tongue. "Very necessary."

Without further delay, Michael kissed her. He tasted of sunshine and birch beer. His lips made no pretext of tentativeness. Instead they boldly captured her lips and snatched her breath away.

Despite his urgency, Michael did not hastily make demands upon her. He progressed at a deliberately provocative pace. Bit by bit he seduced her into his arms until Brittany found herself sandwiched between the unyielding ground beneath her and the beckoning steeliness of Michael's powerful body above her.

Brittany felt his hands caressing her body, gliding over her from shoulder to thigh. He'd never touched her like this before. She made no protest to the hypnotic enticement. Indeed, the light brushing of his palms against the side of her breasts induced the need for more.

Her arms tightened around his neck as she shifted beneath him with beckoning desire. Michael immediately answered her call, his hands abandoning their explorations to undo the buttons of her blouse with smooth efficiency. His mouth left hers to scatter kisses from her chin to her temple, while his hands yielded to temptation and sought the curves of her breasts. Once the front fastening of her bra was released, he ran his hand over her with the supreme confidence of a renegade, pleasuring her even as he sharpened her hunger.

His caresses began at the base of her breast; then, as if tracing an ascending line, his fingers traversed the creamy mound until they reached the firm peak. His skillful manipulations had already aroused her, that much was evident. But Michael wasn't satisfied with that. His mouth stole down her throat to the valley between her breasts. Brittany drew in gasps of breath as he lapped at her with his tongue, as if she were a bowl of cream and he a hungry tomcat.

Her hands slid inside his shirt collar to massage the massive muscles of his shoulders before drawing him even closer. His belt buckle was biting into her hip but she didn't feel the pain. The only pain she felt was caused by the unfulfilled ache deep within her, an ache only he could fill. That ache intensified as Michael continued caressing her breasts. He worked his magic on her with a tongue that was warm and wet and wonderful. After ministering to one tingling peak, he approached the other, taking his time with her.

Brittany was adrift in a world of sensations. But she was abruptly recalled to reality when Michael lowered his hand to her thigh, where his fingers slid beneath her skirt and moved upward with unmistakable intent. She panicked at the idea of going any further. This was not supposed to be happening. Things had gotten out of hand. She had to call a halt before it was too late.

"Stop." She had to repeat the word twice before it sounded like an order rather than a moan.

Michael eased away from her, but only fractionally. "Why?"

"Because I want you to."

He dropped another kiss to her lips. "You don't really mean that."

His confident assumption angered her, and gave her the inducement she needed to resist. "Yes, I do mean it. Now let me up!"

Brittany's anger fueled Michael's. He rolled away from her, rose to his feet, and stood glaring down at her as she still lay, flushed and disheveled, on the blanket. "Make up your mind!" The words were gritty with male frustration. "But don't play the part of a tease by being warm and willing one minute and then cold the next."

"I am not a tease!" she denied while frantically refastening her clothing.

"Come on. I've seen the way you look at me, tasted the way you've returned my kisses, felt the way you melt in my arms.

But you still stubbornly refuse to acknowledge what's going on between us." Michael paused to take a deep breath and impatiently rake a hand through his hair, hair that Brittany's caressing fingers had already rumpled. "I don't know what your problem is, but this hot-and-cold behavior of yours is driving me up a wall. I haven't had a good night's sleep since I took this job." The statement took on the tone of an accusation.

Incensed by his charge, Brittany fairly leapt to her feet. "Nobody asked you to come work at the school, you know! You could have found someone else."

"Who?"

She waved his question aside with an impatient hand. "I don't know — that's your job. You were supposed to have found someone by now. It has been over two weeks. Are you sure you're really trying to find a replacement?"

Michael's expression darkened. "What the hell does that mean?"

"You could be stalling this candidate search so that you can stay on at the school."

"You're crazy!" he told her as he angrily tugged on his boots.

"Am I?"

"Yes."

"Fine." She shrugged. "But I still say you're stalling."

He stiffened at her statement, his green eyes fiery. "Listen, lady, the minute I can rope somebody into taking this security guard job of yours, I'll be more than happy to leave. I've got better things to do with my time."

"I'm sure you do." His last comment hit home. She'd told herself the same thing many times, but hearing it from him made a difference.

"Ah, hell, let's get out of here." Michael gathered up the blanket and the remainder of their lunch.

Without waiting for him, Brittany marched across the field toward the parked motorcycle.

Their return ride was silent and speedy. Luckily, Brittany was still too angry to feel any fear as the countryside raced past them. Her anger was not directed solely at Michael; she was also furious with herself. How could she have let things get so out of control? She was not going to let Michael get to her, she told herself over and over again. She simply couldn't afford to.

CHAPTER SIX

When Brittany arrived at the school on Monday morning, she found two strange cars parked at the curb but no sign of either Michael's motorcycle or his Firebird. Instead there were two men standing in front of the gate leading into the school yard. She cautiously eyed them from within the safe confines of her car. They looked respectable enough; the younger man was dressed in a suit while the other, older man was wearing slacks and a shirt.

Seeing Brittany getting out of her car, the younger man called out to her. "Ms. Evans?"

"That's right." She sent both men a questioning look. "Can I help you?"

"I'm Ray Lewis, from Security Management Systems. We've talked over the phone."

Security Management Systems. Michael's company. Had something happened to him? An accident? Stay calm, Brittany. It's probably nothing. "Good morning, Mr. Lewis."

Ray went on to introduce his companion. "This is Bud Antosiak."

Brittany was really getting worried. "I'm afraid I don't understand . . ."

"Mr. Devlin asked me to bring Mr. Antosiak here this morning for you to interview. We believe you'll be very satisfied with his credentials."

The sun suddenly seemed duller as the reason for the two men's presence became clearer. "I see." So Michael had decided not to return to the school. *Why aren't you relieved?* she silently asked herself. *Wasn't this what you wanted — a permanent guard and no more Michael Devlin to distract you day and night?* The news should have made her feel better, but it didn't. Brittany managed to hide her conflicting emotions behind a smile. "Good morning, Mr. Antosiak. Won't you both please come into my office?"

Brittany led the way through the gate and up the steps to the school's front door, which she unlocked with fingers that shook ever so slightly. Once inside, she almost forgot to deactivate the alarm system before guiding both of her unexpected visitors into the office.

Ray watched her with well-concealed interest. Brittany Evans wasn't at all the way he'd pictured her to be, either from her prior reputation as an ulcer-causing account or from Michael's subsequent description of her. She was a nice-looking woman, to be sure, but a twenty-five on a scale of one to ten? Some of Michael's previous girlfriends had been much better endowed, and had long silky hair. Brittany was slender and had short hair. Her blue eyes were nice, but they dominated a face that was rather thin. Her lips were cute though.

Ray's thorough appraisal of Brittany was completed in the time it took her to sit at her desk. "I have Mr. Antosiak's records right here, if you'd care to look them over." Ray handed the papers to her.

Brittany read them carefully, at least that was the impression she gave. Actually her mind was still trying to adjust to this new twist.

"Would you rather conduct the interview without me?" Ray asked, concerned by her silence.

"No, please stay, Mr. Lewis. You'll have to forgive me, I wasn't expecting you this morning." Brittany locked inside her personal feelings and concentrated on this applicant. According to his employment records, Bud Antosiak was fifty-six, a retired Navy man with security-guard experience who had an impressive history of volunteer work with children. He didn't even look too fierce. In short, the perfect candidate.

Brittany asked Bud Antosiak about his work history, but her questions lacked the biting directness of her usual interviewing techniques. She was only going through the motions, she already knew there was nothing wrong with Bud. He started that morning.

After Ray's departure, Bud brought up the subjects of his weapon and uniform. "I understand that my gun is supposed to be kept in the office safe and that you prefer your guard to wear some sort of a school shirt, is that right?"

"Partially right. Your gun will have to be stored in the safe, yes." Brittany opened the small freestanding safe so that Bud could place his gun inside. After he'd done so, she closed the safe's metal door and handed Bud the combination on a piece of paper, which he placed in his wallet. "As for the uniform, the shirt you have on now will do for today. Otherwise a plain blue shirt with dark slacks will be fine." Anything but that green T-shirt. Brittany didn't want to be reminded of how good Michael had looked wearing that T-shirt.

For the most part, the school's staff members greeted Bud's presence without asking many questions about his sudden appearance. Shelly, however, was the exception.

"Why did Michael leave so abruptly?" she asked Brittany while the other staff members were speaking to Bud. "He didn't even say good-bye."

"You'll have to ask Michael that question," Brittany retorted.

To which Shelly replied, "I'll do that. I'll give him a call."

"Fine." It wasn't, but Brittany had no intention of saying so.

The moment the children began arriving, they immediately noticed Michael's absence and the new guard's presence. What's more, most of the children did not look pleased at the change.

"Who's he?" Kevin asked Brittany with a blunt jerk of his thumb in Bud's direction.

Brittany knew that Kevin's display of bad manners wasn't customary so she didn't reprimand him. "This is our new security guard — Mr. Antosiak."

Kevin did not look impressed. "What happened to Mr. Devlin?"

"Mr. Devlin was only working here temporarily," Brittany replied. "I told you that, remember? Mr. Antosiak is going to be our real guard."

"Where's Mr. Devlin now?" Adam demanded.

"He's gone back to his other job."

"How come? Doesn't he like us anymore?" Maria asked, with tears in her eyes.

"His leaving had nothing to do with not liking you," Brittany hastily assured Maria. "He liked all of you very much."

"Then why did he leave?" demanded Carrie.

"I told you. He had another job to go to."

"Then he likes that other job better than he likes us?" The semibelligerent question was Tiffany's.

Bud came to the rescue. "Actually, Michael and I are friends. He knew how much I like hanging around with kids, so he gave this special job to me, knowing I'd really enjoy it. He told me all about you."

That caught the children's attention, snagging their curiosity. "What'd he tell you?" Adam asked.

"He told me that Daniel likes dinosaurs, that Maria's doll's name is Clarissa, that Matthew's going to grow up to be a scientist —"

Tiffany interrupted him. "My name's Tiffany. What did Mr. Devlin tell you about me?"

"That you're romantic."

"I used to be," Tiffany admitted glumly. "I even tried to get Mr. Devlin to take my mom out." Seeing Brittany's surprised expression, Tiffany defended her actions. "Well, I didn't think you wanted him, so I didn't see why he shouldn't go out with my mom. He'd make a nice dad. But he wouldn't ask her."

"See? Romance stinks!" Kevin declared.

At the moment Brittany tended to agree with him.

Meanwhile, Carrie was stumbling over Bud's surname.

"Mr. Antosiak is a mouthful," he admitted

with a friendly grin. "So if Ms. Evans doesn't mind, I'd like you all to call me Bud."

Brittany gave her approval. "That's fine."

Later that morning Brittany happened to overhear Carrie and Maria talking together.

"Bud's okay," Carrie said, "but I still miss Mr. Devlin."

Maria sighed. "Me too."

Me three, Brittany thought to herself.

Meanwhile, in another corner of the classroom, Kevin, Adam, and Daniel were hatching a plan. "Maybe if we scared this Bud-guy the way we did that other guard, he'll leave and Mr. Devlin will come back." The suggestion came from Kevin.

"You think he's afraid of snakes too?" Daniel asked.

"Could be," Kevin replied. "If not, there's always the ant farm."

"Yeah, that second guy sure got upset when those ants all crawled all over him, under his pants and everything."

"He had ants in his pants!" The three boys giggled conspiratorially at their naughty humor.

"What are you boys up to?" Joan asked them.

"Nothing," they denied in unison.

But Joan had overheard their comment about the ants, and she reported her fears to Brittany. "I'm afraid some of the boys may be planning a little sabotage."

"What do you mean?"

"I have a feeling they may want to get rid of Bud so Michael will come back, the same way they did with those two security guards after Sam's departure."

"Oh, no!"

Joan nodded understandingly.

"For God's sake, keep an eye on the snake," Brittany ordered her. "Chances are that Bud doesn't have the same phobia about snakes that poor man Bruno Maretti did, but we can't take the risk. And the ant-farm trick worked pretty well on that younger guard, so keep an eye on that too."

"You got it."

"I'll talk to the boys."

Brittany did so in the so-called dress-up room at the back of the classroom where fantasies were acted out. At times this room became the deck of a pirate's ship, or the cockpit of a plane, or a space station. For the moment Brittany decided that the room was a security guard's station and that Kevin got to play the part of Bud, the security guard.

For once Brittany joined in the play, taking the role of one of the children. She sat Indian-fashion on the floor. "Let's have some fun," she said in a loud whisper.

"Okay," Adam and Daniel whispered back, smiling expectantly.

But when she said, "Let's scare the

guard," their smiles disappeared.

"We can't do that," they said with an honesty only a five-year-old can lend to a fib.

Brittany pretended to look disappointed. "I suppose you're right. Mr. Devlin would probably be upset if we scared his good friend."

That possibility clearly hadn't occurred to any of the three boys.

But the idea made sense to Kevin. "That's right," he said, really getting into his role as Bud, the security guard. "If you're bad, I'm gonna tell Mr. Devlin on you and he'll come and beat you up."

Daniel took exception to the threat. "Oh, yeah? You do and I'll never let you play with my Star War figures again."

"Kevin was only pretending," Brittany told Daniel. "He didn't mean what he said."

"I don't like this game no more!" Daniel exclaimed. "I want to be Superman."

"No fair!" Adam exclaimed in protest. "You always get to be Superman. This time it's my turn."

"First let's finish the game we're playing here." Brittany's tone was determined. "How do you think Mr. Devlin would feel if he knew you had played a trick on his friend Bud?"

"He'd probably be mad," Adam said.

"Do you think Mr. Devlin would come

back to the school if you played a trick on Bud?"

Adam slowly shook his head. "I guess not."

"What did you like so much about Mr. Devlin?" Brittany found herself asking.

"I dunno," Adam replied. "He kinda looked like Superman."

" 'cept he didn't wear a cape," Daniel added.

Adam nodded. "Yeah, he didn't wear a cape. But he was big and strong."

Kevin inserted his opinion. "He talked to us."

"Don't you think Bud will talk to you?"

"Yeah, I s'pose so. But Bud doesn't look like Superman. Not even if he wore a cape." Kevin shook his head. "He still wouldn't look like Superman."

"Can we play another game now?" Daniel asked.

Brittany nodded. She'd accomplished what she'd set out to do. "We'll bring in the rest of the class and pretend we're all going on a camping trip."

"Okay!"

Within five minutes all fifteen children had gathered around Brittany. "I've got the sack here." She held a make-believe sack in her hands. "What should we bring if we're going to go camping and sleeping outside?"

"A tent," Matthew said.

"Okay." Brittany pantomimed lifting a rolled-up tent and put it into the tall sack. "What else?"

"A flashlight," Carrie said. She was afraid of the dark, so that was a priority item for her.

"Okay. In goes a flashlight. What else?"

The ideas came more rapidly now. As each suggestion was given, Brittany barely had time to place it into the sack before another student shouted his contribution.

"Sleeping bags," said one child.

"Food!" Kevin exclaimed. "Chocolate and —"

"Matches to make a fire," interrupted a third child.

"Pizza!" Kevin continued.

"A knife to protect us from bears and dinosaurs." This, of course, was from Daniel.

"Panty hose!" Tiffany suddenly exclaimed. "You can't go camping without panty hose!"

Brittany put in panty hose.

The make-believe exercise kept the children busy until it was time for them to go home at noon. That afternoon Brittany deliberately pulled out a stack of bookkeeping work that needed to be done. The detailed accounting job required her total concentration and was intended to prevent her from thinking about Michael.

She didn't get a chance to speak with Bud again until the end of the school day. "How was your first day?" she asked him.

"Great."

There was one matter she wanted to check out with Bud for her own peace of mind. "Umm, this may sound like a strange question, Bud, but please humor me. Are you afraid of snakes?"

Luckily, Bud said, "No, not at all."

She tried to sound casual as she asked, "How about ants?"

"No."

Brittany sighed in relief.

"So you don't have to worry," Bud went on to assure her.

"I beg your pardon?"

"Kevin, Daniel, and Adam stopped by my desk after your class this morning. They told me about Bruno and the snake," Bud said matter-of-factly. "They also told me about Johnny and the ant farm. Then they told me that since I was a good friend of Michael's they wouldn't do anything like that to me."

"They didn't actually know that Bruno had a thing about snakes," Brittany quickly explained. "They were just testing him, they weren't deliberately trying to be cruel."

"I figured as much." Bud paused to study Brittany for a brief moment. "Why didn't you ever tell Michael what happened?"

"Bruno begged me not to. He was terribly ashamed of his phobia."

"What about Johnny?"

"The poor man was so embarrassed that I didn't have the heart to broadcast his misfortune. The kids had left the lid off the ant farm and the ants made a beeline for the kitchen. Unfortunately, Johnny was directly in their path and the marauding ants were attracted by his after-shave."

"Doesn't say much for his after-shave, does it?" Bud retorted with a grin.

Brittany produced a smile to match his, her first of the day. "You know, I think you're going to work out fine," she told him with an approving nod. "Where have you been hiding yourself?"

"Michael's been trying to talk me into getting back into the work force for some time now. He told me about this job and the trouble he was having filling the vacancy."

"Have you and Michael been friends for very long?" Brittany was rather proud of the way she casually slipped the question into the conversation.

"Actually I met Michael through my wife, Arlene," Bud replied. "She's his secretary."

"I didn't know that."

"Yeah, she's been with Security Management Systems since the beginning. Anyway, this weekend we got a call from

Michael telling us he really needed to know my decision about applying for this job. I guess it was getting too much for him, holding down two jobs and all."

Brittany had more than a sneaking suspicion that she, not the job, had been the cause of Michael's departure. The knowledge wiped the smile from her face and sent her back into her office to work late.

In another office, a few miles away, Arlene was asking Michael, "Are you okay?" for what he felt had to be the twentieth time that day. Actually it was only the third.

He answered her with impatience. "I'm fine, Arlene, but if you keep asking me, I might not stay fine for very much longer."

"I'm not trying to pry into your personal life —"

"That's a switch."

"— but you did confide in me about your problems with Brittany Evans —"

Michael bristled at her words. "I did not confide."

"— so I can't help but worry about what went wrong between you two."

"Nothing went wrong," he answered impassively. "There was nothing there in the first place."

"That wasn't what you said last week," Arlene pointed out.

"I must have been suffering from burnout last week," Michael muttered. Anticipating

Arlene's protest, he said, "The subject is closed. We've got two weeks' worth of work to catch up on."

During the next two days Michael's mood deteriorated. He'd entered what Arlene labeled as his Heathcliff period, named after *Wuthering Heights*'s silent and brooding hero. Ray and Arlene soon learned to tread lightly in Michael's presence, and complain heartily in his absence.

"What's with him?" Ray asked after Michael had failed to be impressed by the addition of a new account.

"Why ask me?" Arlene retorted. "I'm just the secretary around here."

"Come on, Arlene. Everybody knows that you're an impeccable source of information on the boss. So what gives?"

Unfortunately Michael happened to walk in on them at that moment. Luckily he hadn't overheard Ray's question, but seeing his sales director chatting with Arlene was enough to elicit from him a growling reminder that there was work to be done. Arlene and Ray exchanged a "see-what-I-mean?" look before obeying the edict from their boss.

"He's getting to be impossible," Arlene told her husband over dinner that night. "Romance is one thing, but this is ridiculous!"

"Romance?" Bud questioned as he helped himself to a generous serving of his wife's special whipped potatoes.

"It's love."

Bud looked at his wife in confusion. "They look like potatoes to me."

Arlene, however, was already barreling on to another question. "How about Brittany Evans? What's she been like the past few days?"

"She's been kind of quiet lately," Bud said.

The comment was all Arlene needed to confirm her suspicions. "I knew it!" She smacked her hand on the table.

Bud swallowed his mouthful of pot roast before speaking. "You did? Then why did you ask me?"

Arlene was as excited as her husband was laid-back. "Listen, I think she's got a thing for Michael and I know he's got a thing for her."

"Now, Arlene," Bud warned indulgently. "Don't go getting any matchmaking ideas."

"Well, we can't let them just drift apart this way. They're miserable and they're making all the rest of us miserable."

"Michael's been that bad at work?"

"Worse!" she stated with dramatic emphasis.

"So what do you plan to do about it?"

Arlene immediately corrected Bud's choice of pronouns. "I'm not going to do it, *we* are."

"We are?"

"Yes. Now, here's what I've got in mind . . ."

The remainder of their dinner grew cold as Arlene enthusiastically outlined her game plan.

CHAPTER SEVEN

Operation Cupid, as Bud had teasingly dubbed Arlene's plan, was put into action the very next day — Thursday. Initiating the setup was much easier than Arlene had anticipated. Of course, Michael did give her the perfect opening as soon as she walked into his office.

"Well? Has Bud survived his first four days at Percival School?" he demanded.

Instead of launching into a long reply, as was her wont, Arlene merely nodded and changed the subject. "We have some dictation to get to, sir."

Michael eyed her with sudden suspicion. "Since when have I been *sir?* And since when do you answer a question with only a nod?"

Arlene sat in her chair with professional primness. "I thought you wanted everyone to behave in a more businesslike manner."

"Businesslike, yes. Servantlike, no." Michael studied the tip of his pen with casual interest. "So Bud's got no complaints, huh?"

"About me?" Arlene asked with pretended obtuseness.

"No." Michael glared at her. "About the job. About the school or the people he's working with there."

"No, no complaints," Arlene cheerfully reported. She deliberately let her expression grow slightly melancholy as she softly added, "Of course he did mention . . . but no, you wouldn't be interested in that."

"In what?" Michael demanded.

Arlene played her role of a reluctant confessor beautifully. She looked ready to spill the beans and then paused to shake her head regretfully. "No, I promised you that I wouldn't discuss it and I won't."

Michael was getting exasperated. "When did you promise me you wouldn't discuss it? And what is *it,* anyway?"

"Now, boss, you wouldn't want me to disobey your orders now, would you?"

His patience having long since evaporated, Michael bellowed, "What orders?"

Arlene answered him with exaggerated caution. "About a certain woman whose name you said I wasn't to mention in this office."

Michael took a deep, calming breath before speaking. "I didn't mean that to be taken so literally, Arlene. If Bud is having problems with Brittany Evans, then I want to be informed." Michael tossed his pen onto the organized clutter of his desk and directed his piercing gaze toward Arlene. "I am still the president of this company, and as such, I need to be told about any difficulties my employees encounter."

"Bud isn't having the difficulties," Arlene said.

"Brittany is?"

Arlene nodded.

"With Bud?"

Arlene shook her head.

Michael's patience was waning again. "Come on, Arlene. I know you know how to talk. Quit with all the hints, already, and get to the point!"

"There's no need to get upset, boss," she said in a soothing voice. "Bud just happened to mention that Brittany was acting kind of strange lately."

"So what else is new?" he muttered, half under his breath.

"Then, Brittany was like this before?" Arlene questioned. "That will make Bud feel a bit better. He was worried that her depression might have been caused by something he said."

"Depression?" Michael repeated in astonishment. "What depression?"

Arlene gazed at him innocently and said, "Why, the same depression you said she displayed when you were there."

Michael shook his head. "She wasn't depressed when I was there. Bossy as hell, and impossible, but not depressed."

"Bud says she's been this way ever since he started work on Monday," Arlene added in a deliberately offhand manner.

"I would have thought she'd be thrilled to finally get a permanent guard," Michael murmured.

"Me too." Arlene shrugged. "But instead she seems to be pining for something."

"Pining?" The word caught Michael's attention. "For something or someone? I wonder." He stroked his jaw thoughtfully. "Listen, Arlene, if Bud has anything else to report, you tell me."

Arlene wore her triumphant smile inside. Outwardly she was convincingly casual. "Sure thing, boss."

Bud didn't get his chance to play his role in Operation Cupid until lunchtime. He found Brittany sitting at the kitchen table, a carton of yogurt and a list of some sort in front of her. Bud already knew that Shelly was out running errands, which meant he and Brittany would have the kitchen to themselves.

As he took a seat next to her Bud offered Brittany his standard greeting. "How's it goin'?"

"Could be worse," Brittany absently replied, adding another item to her shopping list. "How about you?"

"I'm worried about Arlene."

Brittany stopped writing and looked at

Bud in concern. "Your wife? Why? Is she ill?"

"No." Bud unwrapped his roast-beef sandwich. "But she's having a hard time at work."

"Oh?" Brittany dipped her spoon into her yogurt. "Why's that?"

Bud shrugged. "Apparently Michael hasn't been acting like himself since he got back to the office on Monday."

"If Michael isn't acting like himself, then who is he acting like?" Brittany asked.

"My wife says he's acting like Heathcliff," Bud replied in a wry voice.

Brittany looked at him in confusion. "Heathcliff?"

Bud made a gesture of incomprehension. "I don't know what she's talking about. She just keeps going on about some English actor, the one who used to do those camera commercials . . ."

"Sir Laurence Olivier?"

Bud nodded. "That's the one. She talks about him and Michael having the same moody and lonely look that Olivier had as Heathcliff. Do you know what she's talking about?"

"I'm not sure, Bud. I know that Laurence Olivier played the role of Heathcliff in the classic movie *Wuthering Heights* with Merle Oberon."

"What would that have to do with Michael?" Bud quickly asked before Brittany could do so.

The clever move put Brittany in the position of having to try and figure out the connection. "Maybe he's got some sort of trouble in his personal life."

"His family's fine," Bud replied. "Arlene already thought of that."

"I was referring to his personal life aside from his family."

"Women, you mean? If Michael was dating anyone steadily, Arlene would know about it. The strange thing is that Michael hasn't dated anyone since he came to work here," Bud recited, just as Arlene had told him to.

"I wonder why not?" Brittany murmured, her expression pensive.

Bud shrugged. "All I know is that Arlene says he's been miserable."

"Is he ill?"

"No. She says he's pining for something."

Something or someone? I wonder? Brittany mused. *No, Michael couldn't be missing her as much as she was missing him. Could he?*

Arlene and Bud repeated their performances on Friday, and then gave the couple the weekend to contemplate what they'd heard.

Stage two of Operation Cupid was put into effect on Monday.

"I think Brittany's waiting for you to call

her," Arlene told Michael after he'd asked if there'd been any more signs of Brittany's depression.

The news surprised Michael. "What makes you think so?"

"Bud says she eagerly answers the phone, as if expecting someone special, and then gets all disappointed. Bud also says that she asks about you a lot."

Now Michael looked pleased. "She does?"

Arlene nodded.

"I see." Michael feigned interest in a stack of papers on his desk. "Well, maybe I will give her a call, just to see how Bud's working out."

Arlene was getting quite good at hiding her triumphant smiles behind a casual facade. "Sounds like a good idea."

For his part Bud had been equally successful with Brittany. Much of Bud's success sprang from the fact that Brittany already missed Michael. No matter how hard she tried to conceal it, that single fact was undeniable. She missed the way he teased her with a grin, the way he devoured her with a look. She even missed the way he glared at her when he was impatient or angry.

So Bud telling her that Michael was experiencing a similar sense of loss was reassuring.

"He seems downright despondent," Bud

said. "We hate to see him like this. But I suppose if Michael were to call you, you probably wouldn't have any interest in speaking with him."

Brittany began to get suspicious. "Did Michael ask you to speak to me?"

Bud refused to look her in the eye. "I'd really rather not say, Brittany," he replied with an abashed expression.

"I understand, Bud." Brittany smiled with sudden satisfaction. Bud's performance convinced her that Michael had indeed asked Bud to speak with her. Before leaving work that day she made it a point to casually say, "If Michael were to call me, I wouldn't be averse to talking to him."

By the time Bud told Arlene, and Arlene told Michael the next morning, the statement went more along the lines of "Brittany's waiting on tenterhooks for your call!"

Michael placed the long-awaited call that very afternoon.

"Percival School, Brittany Evans speaking."

"Brittany, this is Michael."

Just hearing his voice increased her pulse rate and made her own voice softly welcoming. "Hello, Michael."

"I'm calling to see how Bud is working out." The information Michael was relaying might have been work-related, but his inflection made it sound personal.

Brittany responded in kind. "Bud is working out very well. He isn't even too fierce," she added on a teasing note.

"I'm glad to hear that."

The warmth in his voice made her softly say, "The children miss you."

"Do they?" Michael smiled with satisfaction. Thanks to Arlene's guidance, he translated Brittany's sentence to mean that *Brittany* missed him. "How is everyone doing?"

"Daniel and Matthew almost came to blows yesterday over the reality of dinosaurs." She proceeded to give him a condensed version of the incident.

Michael laughed appreciatively. "It sounds like there's a lot going on. Why don't you tell me the rest over dinner?"

"Dinner?" Now it was Brittany's turn to smile with satisfaction. "When?"

"Any night this week."

"Okay." She wrapped the twisted phone cord around her finger with unaccustomed nervous excitement. "I'd like that."

Whereupon Michael immediately asked, "When?"

"Tomorrow night?" she asked, just as quickly.

"Fine. Give me your address and I'll pick you up at seven."

As soon as she hung up Brittany mentally projected what her schedule looked like between now and seven o'clock Friday night. She should have time to fit in a hair appointment with Jean-Pierre, so she called him. Jean-Pierre was indeed able to fit Brittany in and she left his hair salon late Friday afternoon with a softer and slightly curlier version of her original style.

The new look made her feel so good that she splurged and picked up a bottle of a new perfume she'd been eying at the drugstore near her apartment. She also threw in a set of expensive spring-colored eye shadows while she was at it.

Your next assignment is to decide what to wear, Brittany told herself as she stood, still slightly damp from her bath, in front of her neatly organized closet. The slinky dress was tempting — too tempting. She put it back. Her white suit looked great, but she was afraid she'd spill something on it while eating dinner, so that outfit was ruled out.

How about the hot-pink raw-silk skirt? Brittany drew it out and nodded approvingly at the skirt's biased cut, flared skirt, and fashionable length. Thanks to her great organizational skills, the silk tunic top that matched the skirt hung right beside it.

Black accessories and shoes added a touch of drama to the entire ensemble. At the last minute Brittany decided to wear a pair of silky suntan hosiery instead of the lacy black panty hose she'd originally chosen. *There, that was perfect,* she decided as she checked her reflection in the full-length mirror. She leaned closer to recheck her makeup and to clip on a pair of black button earrings before slipping on her strappy black sandals and wandering into her living room to await Michael's arrival.

After opening the sliding glass door leading out onto her own private balcony, Brittany strolled outside. Her apartment faced the waters of Chesapeake Bay and she spoke to the body of water as if it were a person: "Wish me luck tonight."

The sound of her brass door knocker sent Brittany hurrying to the front door. She peered through the security peephole and saw Michael as if through a goldfish bowl. The mere sight of him, distorted though it may have been by the peephole, sent adrenaline surging through her. Her heart beat faster, a flush came to her face, and she felt breathless. All this and she hadn't even let him into her apartment yet!

This is ridiculous, she silently chastised herself. *Michael's the one who's desperate to see you, to spend time with you, so he's probably even more nervous than you are.* The rationalization calmed her.

Actually, Michael was approaching their dinner date with confidence rather than nervousness. The ease with which Brittany had accepted his invitation seemed to indicate that Arlene knew what she was talking about when she'd said that Brittany had been pining for him. If that was true, he planned on being generous and forgiving past misunderstandings. At least that had been his plan until Brittany opened her door and he saw her again. Then all thoughts of plans went out of his head.

Twelve days. It had been twelve whole days since he'd seen her, and yet, looking at her now, Michael suddenly felt as if it had only been twelve seconds. She looked just as good as he'd remembered — maybe even slightly better. Her hair seemed different somehow, although he was no expert on hairstyles. Her eyes, though . . . her eyes were the exact shade of blue he'd seen in his dreams.

Brittany was conducting an equally appreciative visual survey of Michael. He was bigger than she remembered; his shoulders were broader. He'd replaced his jeans with a pair of dark slacks that emphasized the lean length of his legs. But he looked as wonderful as she remembered. His eyes were the exact misty green she'd seen in her dreams.

Brittany looked at Michael; Michael looked at Brittany, and they simultaneously said, "Hi."

Bumping into each other's greetings

broke the ice, making them both smile at their sudden nervousness.

"Are you ready to go?" Michael asked her.

Brittany nodded. They were still standing within a foot of her front door, she realized with a guilty start. She hadn't even invited him in. "Unless you'd like a drink before we leave?"

Michael shook his head. "I've got reservations for seven-thirty, so we'd better get moving."

He was driving the Firebird tonight, thank heaven. His driving was exemplary, no showy moves or speedy takeoffs. The restaurant he took her to specialized in steak dinners. Michael ordered his rare, with both butter and sour cream on his baked potato. Brittany ordered hers medium-well-done with a salad instead of potato.

While waiting for their meal to be served, they began talking about small things. The kids, mostly. But their conversation soon expanded to other topics as they enjoyed their dinner and each other's company. They talked nonstop through dessert and the ride back to Brittany's apartment.

Michael was in the middle of his story about an eccentric client of his when they reached Brittany's front door.

"And then what happened?" she demanded as she took out her key and unlocked her door.

"Am I invited in?" Michael asked before following her inside.

"Of course. You can't leave me in the middle of this story. So go on, you went over to this woman's house to meet her darling Willis . . ."

"Right. She's one of society's grand ladies, so imagine my surprise at discovering that her darling Willis was . . . a dog."

"A dog?"

Michael nodded. "A Pekingese. I told her that we didn't guard animals. She just gave me this frosty look and informed me that she'd read in the papers about my company guarding that outrageous rock group, and if they weren't animals, then she didn't know who was!"

"What did you do?"

"I guarded her darling Willis. He won first prize at the dog show too."

Michael shared in Brittany's laughter.

"I'm glad we spent the evening together," he said in a husky voice.

"So am I," she agreed with a warm smile.

"I had my doubts about calling you . . ."

Brittany was just about to say "I know" when Michael continued, "But when I heard how down you'd been lately, I knew I had to do something."

"Down?" Brittany frowned at him. "I thought you were the one who's been de-

144

spondent." The words were out before she could recall them.

"Me?" Michael looked at Brittany as if she were crazy. "Where did you get an idea like that?"

Disconcerted, she countered, "Where did you get the idea that I was depressed?"

"Probably from the same source that told you I was despondent," Michael murmured with dark displeasure. His face became etched with anger as another idea occurred to him. "You only came out with me tonight to cheer me up?"

Brittany shifted uncomfortably beneath his scrutiny. "Not exactly."

"Then why did you agree to come out with me?"

"I'm not sure," she hedged.

"You're lying." The accusation was softly spoken and gave no warning of his intentions. "I know why you said yes, and so do you." He placed his arms around her. "For this . . ." His last words were muttered against her lips as he kissed her with persuasive thoroughness.

CHAPTER EIGHT

Brittany's will to protest was overridden by her desire for Michael. Surprisingly, his kiss was not demandingly intimate. His old-fashioned restraint pleased her, seducing her into returning the light but persistent pressure of his mouth.

Melting against him, she returned his kiss. Her lips parted, inviting the seducing liberties she knew he was an expert at taking. Her memory was not faulty. By altering the angle of his lips the slightest bit, Michael was able to change the entire texture of the kiss. Where before it had been sweet, now it was passionate. He added brief tongue touches: a light tracing at the corner of her mouth or an inquiring flick to the silken delicacy of the inside of her bottom lip.

Brittany responded with equal imagination, her tongue darting to and fro provocatively. She found his taste and touch to be addictive. Her hands slid over the broad muscles of his back, loving the feel of his warm skin through the smooth cotton.

Michael's arms tightened around her as

his kisses strayed across her face to the tiny pulse beating at her temple. So, too, did his hands stray, from the small of her back around to the vulnerable sides of her breasts, where he fondled her with skillful sensitivity. His touch brought her to life and she felt a sense of wonder at this heavenly current singing within her.

"You see what we have going between us?" Michael whispered in a voice made raspy by desire. "Feel what you do to me." Widening his stance, he nudged his knee between hers, and then shifted her body so that she was pressed up against him.

His actions intensified the intimacy of their embrace, making her very much aware of his arousal. "Oh, Michael!" She spoke his name in a voice that fell somewhere between a sigh and a moan.

Her breathing was fast and shallow as Michael's hands slid beneath her silk tunic to caress her. The feel of his touch on her bare skin was electrifying. Aching to touch him with equal intimacy, Brittany tugged his shirt from the waistband of his slacks. Now she was free to enjoy the feel of his warm flesh and hard muscles without the protective covering of his shirt.

He felt so good — so strong, so powerful. Eager to explore more of him, her unsteady hands attacked the buttons on his shirt until it hung open, inviting further exploration. She ran her palms across the hard ridges of his ribs. But when she reached the quivering tautness of his abdomen, Michael captured her adventuring hand and abruptly put some distance between his body and hers.

His expression was one of raw restraint, his green eyes dark with desire as he murmured, "Lady, unless you're prepared to go all the way with this, we'd better stop right here."

Brittany stared at him, blinking myopically before gathering her shattered senses. Reality rushed in on her. She'd done it again, responded to him with a wantonness that might easily lead Michael to believe she was ready to go to bed with him. "I'm sorry," she murmured unsteadily.

With a regretful sigh Michael rebuttoned his shirt and stuffed it back into his trousers. "Sorry I kissed you or sorry you can't go to bed with me?"

The question was too complicated for Brittany to answer in her present state. She walked to the couch on trembling legs and gratefully sank onto the upholstered cushions before speaking. "Okay, I admit it. We're dynamite together. But you have to admit that we don't know each other very well."

Michael didn't admit a thing. Instead he ambled over to her overstuffed easy chair and sat down in his favorite position — legs stretched out and crossed at the ankles. He looked very much at home, and not at all as if he'd just been in the midst of a sizzling love scene a few moments ago. "What do you want to know?"

Put like that, Brittany didn't quite know how to reply. In the first place, she was envious of his quick recovery. Her nerve endings were still quivering. What *did* she want to know about him? "Your background. Tell me about your background."

"I grew up in a working-class neighborhood of Baltimore. My folks still live there. I come from a large family, but then you already know that."

She nodded, remembering jotting a note about his large family on the margin of his résumé the first day she'd met him.

"My dad was a security guard, so I guess you could say I've followed in his footsteps. He's had some trouble with his back these past few years, so he's not working full-time anymore. Anyway, I got the idea of running a security service when I got laid off. The company I'd been working for was fairly small and they just couldn't afford the position of a guard anymore. Not that my salary was anything to brag about, far from it, but when they added in their share of social security payments, health insurance, and other benefits, it added up." Michael shrugged. "I figured other small businesses had to be in the same bind so I started Security Management Systems. How about you?"

"Me?"

"How about your background?"

Brittany gave him the bald facts. "I grew up here in Annapolis. My parents got divorced when I was very young. My mother remarried and she's living in London now."

"No brothers or sisters?"

She shook her head. "I guess that's why I like kids so much, I missed out on that part of growing up. Did you enjoy having so many brothers and sisters when you were a kid?"

"I suppose so. The worst thing was waiting for your turn in the bathroom. We had only one."

Brittany had to smile at his prosaic perspective. "Listen, would you like some coffee or something?"

"Coffee sounds good," he replied.

"I'll go make some." She welcomed the opportunity to do some busywork.

"Need any help?" Michael shouted his question toward the café doors through which Brittany had disappeared.

"No, thanks," she shouted back while pouring coffee grounds into the filter of her automatic coffee maker. "Do you take yours black or with cream and sugar?"

"Sugar, no cream."

Preparing the coffee helped calm her nerves somewhat, and she felt more in control by the time she brought out their two cups.

Michael waited until she was seated before asking, "What are you doing tomorrow?"

"Running some errands in town. Why?"

"You claim we don't know each other very well. There's only one way that I know of to remedy that. Spending time together. Starting tomorrow. We can run your errands together."

"If that's what you'd really like to do . . ."

"What I'd really like to do is take you to bed and make wild, passionate love to you."

Brittany almost choked on her coffee.

"Why the surprised look?" Michael asked. "You know how I feel about you. It's no secret."

She looked away from him.

"You're not used to plain speaking, is that it?"

Suddenly Brittany was too tired to argue the point so she sipped her coffee instead of replying.

"No argument? A sure sign of exhaustion," he diagnosed before setting his now empty coffee cup back on its china saucer. "What time do you want me to pick you up tomorrow?"

"Ten would be fine."

"I'll be here." He got up but motioned her to remain seated. "No, don't see me out. I can find my own way." Before leaving he took a short detour over to the couch and dropped a butterfly kiss on the top of her head. "See you tomorrow."

When Michael brought his motorbike the next morning, Brittany was less than thrilled.

Seeing her expression, Michael explained his reasoning. "The bike will be easier to park in the center of Annapolis. You did say that that's where you had to run most of your errands, didn't you?"

"Yes."

"Well, then." He smiled at her, clearly expecting her to congratulate him on his brilliance. "This is the perfect answer."

Brittany remained doubtful. "I don't know about that."

"You're already dressed for the part," he said, sending an admiring look at her well-fitted slacks.

"It seems sacrilegious somehow to be riding a motorcycle in the midst of a bona fide historical landmark," she protested. In fact, the heart of Annapolis had changed so little since the eighteenth century that the entire downtown area had been designated a National Historical Landmark.

"I wasn't planning anything radical like

doing wheelies inside the State House or anything," Michael assured her as he slipped the helmet over her head.

"I should hope not," she retorted. "Our State House is the country's oldest state capitol in continuous use. The Treaty of Paris ending the Revolutionary War was ratified there, you know."

"No, I didn't know." He fastened the helmet's chin straps for her. Then, adding a gentle tap to her nose, he told her, "You look cute."

She grimaced. "Cute?"

"I think cute is sexy."

As Brittany held on to Michael during the brief ride downtown, she decided that *he* was sexy, even if he was too masculine ever to be described as cute. Riding behind him, her arms completely encircled his waist, and her legs rested against the backs of his thighs. She liked holding him and actually felt regret when the short ride was over.

Michael was right, the motorcycle's compact size did make finding a parking space easier. They located one on Main Street, right in the middle of town. Michael had to smile as he watched Brittany take out a neat list itemizing all her errands. Such organization!

Their first stop was a card shop. As they passed a couple of Naval Academy students, Michael asked Brittany, "Whatever happened to your Ivy Leaguer officer?"

"Nothing happened to him as far as I know." Brittany began browsing through the selection of cards. "I haven't seen him since the school's Spring Festival."

"That's good."

"It is?"

"Sure." Michael reached over to stroke her cheek. "That means I don't have to fight him off."

The sound of a child yelling Brittany's name prevented her from replying.

"Ms. Evans! Ms. Evans!"

Two girls came running up to Brittany and hugged her excitedly.

"You know these kids?" Michael mouthed at Brittany as she looked at him over the girls' shoulders.

Brittany nodded and made the introductions. "Michael, this is Kay and this is May Ling. They are both former students of mine."

The girls smiled at Michael and then launched into a detailed listing of their recent activities.

It seemed to Michael as if he'd barely extracted her from those two kids' eager clutches when Brittany was recognized again in the next store, this time by a mother and her seven-year-old son.

"I'm sorry," Brittany apologized to Michael as they left the gift shop twenty minutes later. "I don't usually run into so many of my former students."

"All this recognition. It's worse than being with a famous actress," Michael complained in a dramatic voice.

"Oh? How many famous actresses have you been with?" she demanded suspiciously.

Michael just grinned. "Your jealousy is showing again."

"I'm not jealous," she denied. "Merely curious."

"You know what they say about curiosity and the cat."

"You know what they say about men who avoid questions," she retorted.

"Does it have something to do with snakes or ant farms?"

Michael's mocking comment stopped her in her tracks. "You know!"

He nodded.

"How long?"

"Bud told me. He said that you hadn't sworn him to secrecy, and he thought it was time that the whole thing was cleared up."

"Did he explain to you that the children had no idea Bruno was so fearful of snakes?"

"He explained, about the entire thing. Including the popularity of Johnny's aftershave with the ant population."

"It wasn't a laughing matter at the time, I can assure you."

"Just think, if those ants hadn't attacked Johnny, I might not have met you."

The idea of never having met Michael gave Brittany a strange feeling in the pit of her stomach. She tried to pass it off as hunger. "How about lunch? My treat."

"Why your treat?"

"You treated last night."

Michael took her hand as they reached the busy intersection near the docks. "I'm the man, I'm supposed to treat."

"Look, if it will make you feel any better, I'm not offering you an expensive five-course meal. Just a simple sandwich and soda."

By this time they'd reached the Market House, a restored nineteenth-century building that housed a variety of food stands selling everything from pizza to freshly caught shrimp. Brittany proceeded directly to one stand in the corner and ordered two lobster-salad sandwiches on Kaiser rolls and two birch beers.

"You call lobster salad a simple sandwich?" Michael asked in an undertone as they waited for their sandwiches to be made.

"I'm sorry. That's their specialty. I thought you'd like it, but if you'd prefer something else . . ."

"I'm only kidding. Lobster salad will be fine."

It was fine. In fact, the sandwich was delicious, and Michael grandly proclaimed it to be so as they sat on a bench facing the city docks and ate their carry-out lunch. The good weather had brought out tourists and natives alike and the Colonial downtown area was bustling with people.

"Let's walk back up Cornhill Street," Brittany suggested once they'd finished eating and disposed of their trash. "I love looking at those old Colonial homes being restored."

Apparently a number of other people also loved looking at the historical houses, because the area was almost as crowded as the center of town had been.

Brittany learned that Michael didn't like crowds. And, as they passed by a trellis of fragrant blossoms, Michael learned that Brittany had a soft spot in her heart for wild honeysuckle. This was just one of the many discoveries they made during the next two weeks.

They spent all their free time together, sometimes going out, sometimes staying in for a quiet evening at Brittany's apartment. One Saturday in early May Michael informed her that he knew of a great place to watch the sunset.

"Where?" Brittany asked.

"I'll show you."

By now Brittany was becoming accustomed to Michael's surprises, and she had to confess that she'd enjoyed all of them, from the heart-shaped Mylar balloons he'd given her to the all-night deli they'd visited.

It didn't take Brittany long to realize that they were heading west on U.S. 50, which led directly to Washington, D.C. Upon their arrival in the city, Michael maneuvered through the capital's notorious traffic with ease. He took Brittany past the White House before heading for their final destination.

"This is a good place to watch the sunset?" Brittany asked once they'd parked and begun walking toward one of the capital's most famous sights. "The Lincoln Memorial?"

"Trust me. There's nothing like it." Michael threaded his fingers through hers as he confessed, "Besides, I had an ulterior motive."

"And what might that be?"

"Getting you away from your students. I don't want to be constantly reminded that you're a teacher."

His comment irked her. "What's wrong with my being a teacher?"

Michael soothed her ruffled feathers. "Nothing. I think you're a wonderful teacher. But I also think you're a sexy woman and it's the sexy woman I'd like to get to know better. But it's a little hard to do that with kids running up to you wherever we go." His grin was slightly self-conscious as he said, "I guess I'm just not used to a kindergarten teacher looking like you. Mine sure didn't. Mrs. Bloom was her name and torture was her game. She never smiled. She must have been eighty if she was a day."

"She was probably thirty-two and just looked older from having taught kids like you every day."

Michael laughed at her sharp retort. "What makes you think I was a troublemaker as a kid?"

"The fact that you're a troublemaker now."

"Me? Hey, I'm the calmest member of my family," he retorted. "You know — the shy, quiet one."

"Ms. Evans!" a child's voice cried. "Ms. Evans!"

"I don't believe it!" Michael groaned.

"Oh, no," Brittany muttered, having spotted the child who was frantically waving at her. "It's Tiffany."

"What's she doing here?" Michael demanded.

"How should I know? But she's going to report everything she sees to the rest of the class, so no funny-business," Brittany warned him.

159

"I left my Groucho Marx act at home," Michael mumbled out of the side of his mouth even as he was smiling at Tiffany.

"Mr. Devlin!" she exclaimed, almost out of breath from her race to catch up with them. "It's me, Tiffany. Do you remember?"

"Of course I remember. You're a long way from home."

"Not really, my mom's right over there." She pointed to a woman talking to a tall, dark man before shifting her attention back to Michael. "Hey! You're holding hands!"

"That's so I don't get lost," Michael told Tiffany in a confidential whisper.

Tiffany giggled.

"Ms. Evans is going to show me the Lincoln Memorial," he went on to say.

"Really? She already showed it to us, last year. Course we were just kids then, but I wanted my mom to see it too. I didn't know they let teachers come here without kids," Tiffany added as an afterthought.

"Tiffy, where are you?" her mother called.

"Oh, oh. I gotta go. See ya!"

As Tiffany ran toward her mother, Michael tugged Brittany off in the opposite direction. "Come on. Tiffany's mother is a real barracuda, I'd rather not run into her again. Besides, we've got to hurry or we'll miss the sunset."

This was the first time Brittany had seen the Lincoln Memorial at twilight. The sky was just turning that washed-out white that precedes a sunset. Up the wide staircase, past the Doric columns, could be seen the amber glow that bathed the massive seated statue of Lincoln done by David Chester French.

As Michael and Brittany patiently waited, the sky began to glow. Slowly, almost imperceptibly, a diffuse crimson light shone upward like a rising wall of color, steeping the thin cirrus clouds with a rosy hue. The glorious show lasted only a few brief moments before fading.

It was then that the floodlights went on, lighting the memorial as impressively as the sun had lit the twilight sky. Elsewhere in the city other landmarks came to life in the encroaching night. From where Michael and Brittany stood at the top of the Lincoln Memorial's steps, they could see the illuminated obelisk of the Washington Memorial mirrored in the Reflecting Pool and, farther on, the Capitol building. It felt as if the city of Washington lay at their feet, luminous and unforgettable.

"Neat, huh?" Michael asked in a soft voice.

"Spectacular," Brittany murmured.

"Want to see the view from the back?"

"There's more?"

Michael nodded and slipped his arm around her shoulders as they walked around the portico. From the back of the monument they could see the Arlington Memorial Bridge spanning the Potomac River. And, in the distance, Arlington National Cemetery, where both President and Senator Kennedy were buried.

"Do you know the name of that building over there, the one that's lit up on that hill above the cemetery?" Michael lifted his hand from her shoulder to point out the building he meant.

"That's the Custis Lee mansion, home of Robert E. Lee, the commander in chief of the Confederate Army," Brittany replied. "During the Civil War the government confiscated Lee's home and the surrounding property for nonpayment of taxes. Union soldiers had already begun burying their dead on the slopes beyond the house so they turned that part of the estate into a cemetery."

"I figured you'd know what it was, you being a teacher and all." Michael delivered the compliment in a teasingly humble voice.

Brittany teased him in kind. "So there are times when my being a teacher comes in handy, hmm?"

"Mmm, but if we're getting *handy*" — his fingers stroked the curve of her cheek — "then the teacher can take a break and the sexy lady can come out and play."

The look in his green eyes made Brittany

forget the other visitors milling around them. He spoke to her in a language that needed no words. When his fingers strayed to the corner of her mouth, Brittany pouted her lips into a kiss over which Michael's index finger skimmed. The tip of her tongue flicked out to taste his skin.

"Let's go home." The words came from Michael, the thought from Brittany.

Her eyes were dreamy, her plans seductive during the return trip to Annapolis. This night was special. The moon seemed softer, the stars closer.

When they arrived at her apartment Michael came in for a nightcap. Brittany broke open a bottle of Kahlua and a package of tiny cup-shaped Godiva chocolates. The set had been a birthday present from the parents of one of her students and Brittany had been saving it for a special occasion. Something told her tonight was it.

She poured the coffee-flavored liqueur into the fluted cups and set them on a tray, which she carried out onto the balcony, where Michael was already seated. The outdoor temperature was balmy, the breeze light.

"What's this?" Michael asked as he took the tray from her and set it on a small redwood table.

"Dessert." They'd already eaten an early dinner before they'd gone to Washington.

Picking up one of the cups, he sniffed it suspiciously. "What's in here?"

"A surprise. Go on, drink it, it won't poison you."

"Do you drink it or eat it?"

Now that Brittany thought about it, she wasn't sure what the proper procedure was. "I suppose you could do either." She chose to sip the liqueur from the chocolate cup.

Michael popped the entire thing in his mouth and crunched contentedly, making "mmm" sounds of approval.

His approach looked like so much fun that Brittany ate her next one that way. There was something strangely sensuous about blending the hard chocolate with the warm liquid.

Since Brittany had only one redwood chaise lounge, both she and Michael were seated on it. As time went by Brittany didn't know whether it was the liqueur or Michael's nearness that was making her feel so delightfully giddy. But the moment Michael kissed her, she knew he was the reason she felt as though she had champagne bubbles in her bloodstream. This intoxication was not alcohol-induced, but passion-provoked.

One kiss led to another, and another. As if blown by the gentle night breeze, Michael and Brittany drifted down into a horizontal position on the lounge chair. Lack of space dictated that they lie on their sides, facing each other.

Michael's leg shifted until it rested atop hers, pinning her to the chaise lounge. Instead of protesting the increased intimacy of their embrace, Brittany enhanced it by sliding her left hand behind his bent knee and pulling him closer. Her clothed body then rubbed against his in silky little strokes that set them both on fire.

Meanwhile Brittany's right hand was alternately rifling through Michael's hair or teasing the curve of his ear while her lips pressed tiny kisses across his jaw. Michael responded by first capturing her wayward lips in a consuming kiss. Then his hands descended over her back to the downward slope of her denim-clad bottom, where he cupped her to him. Lifting her against him, he skillfully increased the rhythmic rubbing of their hips.

The ecstasy soon turned to agony as, with each sensual sweep, the leashed power in Michael grew until it reached a point of acute need. Tearing his lips away from hers, he groaned, "Lady, this is your last chance. Any more of this and I'm not going to be able to stop."

Brittany's lips turned upward into a smile of blatant invitation as her hand traversed downward over his chest and abdomen with an even bolder and infinitely more direct reply. She skated one fingernail down the taut zipper placket of his jeans before covering him with the heart of her palm. The look of intense pleasure on his face reinforced her decision.

"Don't stop!" They both whispered the words at the same time.

"I won't stop," Brittany promised in a throaty voice, caressing him again.

"I *can't* stop," Michael growled. "So we'd better get off this balcony and into bed before I take you right here!"

Breathing unsteadily, he surged to his feet before bending over and pulling her up to join him. Her eyes, glazed with desire, were the darkest blue he'd ever seen. A man could drown in those eyes, drown in that body — and he intended to do so. Impatient now of the distance between them, he lifted her into his arms.

She nestled against him like a contented cat. "My bedroom's down the hall on the right," she whispered, punctuating her instructions by blowing into his ear and nibbling his earlobe.

Michael's long stride ate up the distance between the balcony and the bedroom with the efficiency of a runner. She could feel the beat of his heart against the vulnerable side of her breast as the cadence of his stride rocked her against him.

Once they reached her bedroom he made

no move to place her on the bed. Instead he let her slide against his fully aroused body as he set her on her feet. Then he kissed her.

As her mouth eagerly merged with his, her bare feet curled into the plushness of her bedroom carpet. Only then did Brittany vaguely realize that she must have lost her shoes somewhere along the way. Not that it mattered, nothing mattered but Michael. She uncurled her toes and stood on tiptoe to further meet the demands of his tempting tongue. Michael rewarded her by nibbling on her bottom lip in a way he knew she loved.

As her fingers stealthily unbuttoned his shirt Michael's fingers were busy unfastening the pearly buttons of her blouse. These maneuvers called for some space between them, and it soon became a challenge to continue their kiss under such circumstances. They both laughed huskily as they met the challenge, each refusing to relinquish the other's lips.

When Brittany opened her eyes she discovered that Michael's eyes weren't closed either, for he was gazing down at her with undeniable enjoyment. Looking at the magnificent man standing before her brought a new sensual dimension into play and made the temporary cession of their kiss easier to accept. In perfect unison Michael slid

Brittany's blouse off one shoulder just as she was sliding his shirt off his shoulder.

Watching him watching her was unexpectedly exciting. She saw the way his eyes rested upon each inch of her skin as he exposed it, as if he were drinking in the very sight of her. She smiled at him and observed him with equal relish. Her eyes slid over his tanned skin in a way that left him in little doubt as to her thoughts.

"At last!" Brittany murmured in triumph, tossing his shirt onto a chair in the corner of her room.

"That's supposed to be my line," Michael murmured as he let her blouse drift to the floor.

She eyed him as if he were a present and she were the one who got to unwrap him. "What shall I work on next?" she asked flirtatiously.

"I've got a few suggestions."

"Tell me, I'm all ears," she said in a breathy little voice.

"You don't look all ears."

"No?"

"No. Not that they aren't nice ears," he assured her with husky sincerity. His tongue touched her earlobe before swirling inside her ear. "Very nice." She both heard and felt his words.

"Mmmm, very nice." The way she repeated his words sounded very much like a feline purr. In keeping with her catlike image, Brittany licked her way across the bare expanse of his muscular chest.

She loved the way his skin tautened beneath her teasing tongue. It made her feel gloriously powerful and feminine.

Michael expanded his explorations from her ear down the column of her neck to the base of her throat. His dalliance there made her fingers unsteady as she attempted to unfasten the snap on his jeans.

Michael's fingers had developed a similar unsteadiness as he attempted to unfasten the snap on her jeans.

As if on cue they suddenly looked at each other and grinned.

"You take care of yours, and I'll take care of mine," she suggested.

"Deal."

As a result of their decision, their trousers were shucked in a quarter of the time it had taken them to remove each other's shirts.

"That was much more efficient," Brittany murmured, suddenly feeling ridiculously nervous.

"But not half as much fun." Michael paused a moment before saying softly, "You're gorgeous."

Brittany stood before him, garbed in two flimsy articles of lingerie. Her bra and lacy panties were both delectable confections, all dim and rosy in the moonlight streaming in from the uncovered windows.

Sensing her nervousness, Michael stood his ground and opened his arms to her. At first Brittany moved toward him with shy little steps. But as she got closer to him, and saw the emotion radiating from his eyes, her steps became surer and more confident until she entered his embrace as an equal partner.

"I haven't done this very often." Her rueful confession was voiced against the section of his throat that was directly beneath his right ear.

"No?" He combed his fingers through her hair with soothing tenderness. "I'm glad."

"You are?"

He nodded before confessing, "I have this possessive streak a mile long where you're concerned."

Brittany couldn't resist leaning away from him and murmuring in awe, "A mile long?"

He delivered a playful swat to her fanny. "Not much experience, huh? That didn't sound like an innocent question to me."

Brittany returned the swat. "I'm a quick study."

"Mmm, well there won't be anything quick about tonight. It's taken us long enough to get here. I want to make the most of this."

Despite her bold words, Brittany's breath caught in her throat as his mouth sought the soft swell of her breast. His feathering tongue probed her through the sheer material of her bra. Like a shot of raw electricity, pleasure swept through her, nearly buckling her knees. Both her hands sank into the thick vibrancy of his hair as she held him to her.

Reaching around her, Michael slowly unfastened her bra and removed it. Brittany gleefully celebrated the lack of material barriers by brushing her breasts against his bare chest. Now it was Michael's turn to go weak at the knees as the thrusting tips of her breasts drove him to distraction.

Brittany's hands, which were resting at his waist, moved around to the small of his back, where her nails raked bewitching little circles across his flesh. With a raspy groan, Michael backed her up to the bed. Bracing one knee on the mattress, he lowered her to the comforter without releasing her from his tight embrace.

He lay over her like a blanket. Brittany shivered with excitement as he peeled away the remaining articles of clothing from first her body and then his. Pausing, he suddenly gazed down at her with something nearing uncertainty.

Brittany couldn't understand why. He was glorious — so solid, so strong. Her hands moved over him with tentative appreciation, tracing the pattern of crisp hair

171

from his navel to . . .

"Honey, wait." The words were torn from his throat.

Her hands stopped roving. "Why?"

"I'm not using any protection." His voice was ragged with passion.

"I am," she murmured.

Her words erased the last sign of uncertainty from Michael's face. He gathered her to him, his hands coasting up and down her spine as if memorizing the feel of her. But their growing mutual need was such that the time for leisurely explorations was fast reaching an end.

Accordingly, Michael's caresses became increasingly intimate until they focused on the one spot that ached for attention. There he propositioned her with a sensual simulation of what was yet to come. Displaying skillful precision, Michael ministered to her needs even as he fueled her hunger. Wave upon wave of delicious sensation buffeted her.

Fearful of traversing this sensual trip without Michael, she reached for him and guided him to her. He was firm and ready; she was warm and willing. He came to her in seductive stages — the introduction, the erotic dalliance, and then . . . the final possession. Brittany enveloped him, eagerly absorbing all that he offered her.

"Oh, honey, you feel so good," he groaned.

"So do you," she was able to gasp before his gliding thrusts drove her on to a dizzying peak of excitation where words were useless and the undulations of passion prevailed.

Michael's rhythm was exquisitely measured. Slower, then faster, then slower again. He drank her moans of pleasure as he regulated the speed of his thrusts. Brittany moved with him, initiating a flowing cadence of her own.

Michael's body tensed as he fought for control. But Brittany had obviously had enough of control. Her response was wildly passionate and wantonly abandoned.

Smiling with devilish surrender, Michael reached between them and performed one last rite of magic. Brittany had a brief sensation of being suspended in midair before her entire being expanded and contracted in ever-increasing pulses of satisfaction. Her fulfillment hastened his own, and sent him hurtling through space with her.

In the hazy aftermath of their lovemaking Brittany lay cradled against Michael. Although no words were spoken, communication flourished, transmitted through caresses that were rich with emotion. And when Brittany eventually drifted off to sleep, she curled trustingly into the warmth of the man who lay beside her.

CHAPTER NINE

There's a man in my bed. The drowsy realization was Brittany's first conscious thought the next morning. His name permeated her mind. *Michael.* Turning on her side, Brittany propped herself up on one elbow in order to better study him.

He looked earthy and sexy sprawled out on the dainty pastel-colored bottom sheet. At some time during the night he'd kicked aside the top sheet. With nothing to interrupt her view, Brittany could see how well built Michael's body truly was. She tried selecting a suitable adjective to describe his physique. Solid? Sturdy? She shook her head. Those words made him sound like a tree trunk or a piece of furniture. Not the living and breathing work of art he was.

As her loving gaze slid over Michael's sleeping form, Brittany felt like stamping MINE over every inch of him. He slept facedown into the pillow, no doubt burrowing away from the sunlight pouring in through the still-uncovered bedroom window. His sun-streaked hair was rumpled so invitingly that she was unable to resist reaching out to softly caress it.

Michael shifted in his sleep but didn't awaken. She could see his face now. His lips were curved in a smile of satisfaction. Brittany smiled herself, confident in the knowledge that she was the one who'd put that smile on his face.

She thought back over the time they'd spent together during the past few weeks. Like someone poring over a favorite photograph album, she touched upon all the little things she'd learned about Michael. She knew he liked his coffee with sugar and no cream. She knew he preferred driving his motorcycle to his car. She knew how long he'd owned his favorite pair of jeans and that he hated vinegar.

She also knew that she loved Michael Devlin. She shouted the words, silently, within herself. Part of her wanted to wake Michael and share the news with him. But that other part of her feared rejection. He'd said he wanted her, but that didn't necessarily mean he wanted her love as well.

Michael used words sparingly, she knew that. She also knew her strong and silent man wasn't the type to use the word *love* lightly. But if he said it, he would mean it. For that, Brittany was willing to wait.

Meanwhile, she felt no regrets at what they'd shared throughout the night. For now she was content to simply enjoy the fact that they'd found each other. And she wanted to celebrate it.

Careful not to wake Michael, she slipped out of bed. She wanted to surprise him with breakfast in bed. Dressed in a peach silk robe, she padded into the kitchen on bare feet and quietly set about preparing the best gourmet breakfast ever made. The menu consisted of an omelet-type concoction, with artichoke hearts, mushrooms, and cheese, called a frittata, plus bacon, freshly squeezed orange juice, and hot coffee.

As she performed her culinary labors she came across a spider meandering its way across her no-wax kitchen floor. Brittany was no more eager to live with a spider than the next person, but she was also very squeamish about squishing insects. It seemed easier for her to just scoot them outside rather than kill them.

Picking up the sheet of cardboard she kept for just such a purpose, Brittany began shooing the octoped out of the kitchen and onto the tiled foyer floor leading to her front door. She knew from past experience that spiders didn't shoo well on plush carpeting, so she didn't lead it through the living room over to the balcony door even though that was closer.

This spider was more stubborn than most, however, so she began issuing verbal instructions to it, in a quiet whisper so as not to wake Michael. "Come on, hurry up, I haven't got all day."

"What are you doing?" Michael asked from directly behind her bent-over figure.

Brittany straightened with a speed that made her light-headed. "There's a spider . . ."

"Want me to kill it?" he offered, moving closer.

"No!" She waved him back.

"No? You save spiders?"

"No. Yes . . . I'm trying to get him to go outside," she explained, keeping her eyes on the crafty spider. "I don't want him in my apartment but I don't want him dead."

"What makes you think this spider is a male?"

Brittany didn't answer Michael's teasing question, there wasn't time. "He's getting away!" She opened her front door a few inches and bent over again, carefully using the sheet of cardboard as a nudge. "Hurry up, get outside. You'll like it out there," she assured the spider. "It's sunny and warm today and you'll probably meet some other nice spiders out there." As if listening to her words, the spider suddenly scuttled its way to freedom.

Brittany closed the front door after it and leaned back against the portal, closing her eyes in relief. "Finally! I thought he'd never leave."

Michael just looked at her and said, "I think I'm in love with a woman who chases spiders out her front door."

Joy spread through her. Her eyes flew open to search his face with a hopeful gaze. "Really?"

Michael nodded gravely. "Really."

The one word was all the assurance Brittany needed. She threw herself into his arms with jubilant abandon. "I'm so glad!" She showered a mixture of hugs and kisses upon him.

Michael returned her hugs and kisses with equal enthusiasm. "Does this mean you feel the same way?" he whispered in her ear.

"I love you." She said the words against his bare throat. "I love you," she repeated against his bare chest. "I . . . you're not wearing any clothes!"

"You just noticed?" he complained in a grumbly voice. "I'm devastated."

Brittany stepped back far enough to allow her eyes to sweep over him. "Devastating is more like it," she said in a husky voice that conveyed her delight.

Michael grinned even as a hint of color tinged his face. Tugging her back into his arms, he unwrapped her silk robe and slid it down her arms. He then proceeded to kiss his way from her left to her right shoulder. The trip took him awhile because he paused frequently at her mouth and, when he did so, Brittany made the most of the opportunity by plying his lips with her tantalizing tongue.

Sometime later Michael lifted his head to murmur, "Something's burning."

"Me," she whispered, melting against him only to jump away a second later. "Oh, no! My frittata!"

"Your what?"

But Brittany was already in the kitchen, grabbing pans and wailing, "It's ruined!"

"What was it?" Michael asked, warily eying the charred remains.

"Frittata. I was going to impress you and serve you a gourmet breakfast in bed. So much for that idea." Flipping open her garbage can, she dumped in the entire contents of the frying pan.

"The bacon's fine," he told her after munching on a slice he'd snitched from a paper-towel-covered plate.

As soon as she set the pan into the sink, Michael snared her in his arms again. "Besides, I can think of a lot of other ways for you to impress me in bed. Ways that are a lot more fun than eating breakfast."

Brittany looped her arms around his neck. "Really?"

"Really. Here, let me show you." Scooping

her up in his arms, he carried her back to the bedroom and did indeed show her. Show her how much he loved her, how much he wanted her.

The memory of their lovemaking still had the power to send shivers up and down her spine at work on Monday. Those shivers were exacerbated by the shrill giggles and squeals her students were issuing that morning, a sure sign they were excited.

"Is it true?" Daniel was yelling above the other voices. "Is it true?"

"Is what true, Daniel?" Brittany asked in a calm voice.

"What Tiffany says," Daniel answered. "She says she saw you and Mr. Devlin."

"Together!" Adam added.

"Holding hands!" Carrie tacked on.

"It's true that Tiffany saw me with Mr. Devlin. We were at the Lincoln Memorial in Washington." Hoping to distract the children, she said, "You all remember the Lincoln Memorial, don't you? We visited it last October."

"Was that the building that looks like a wedding cake?" Carrie asked.

"Yeah, that's where Superman lives," Adam inserted. "You can see him sittin' on a chair."

"That's Abraham Lincoln, Adam," Brittany told him. "Not Superman."

"Are you sure?" he demanded.

"Positive," Brittany replied.

"Oh." Adam came up with an alternative story. "Then Superman must live underneath that building where no one can see him."

"I want to talk about Mr. Devlin," Maria stated, tugging on Brittany's slacks. "Is he coming to see us?"

Brittany smiled down at the little girl. "I don't know, Maria. He's awfully busy with his job."

"He saw you, didn't he?" Maria pointed out.

"Yes."

"Then how come he can't see us?"

Brittany couldn't fault Maria's logic. "Maybe he can. I'll ask him, okay?"

Maria grinned. "Okey-dokey." The phrase was the newest addition to her vocabulary.

Brittany got her chance to speak to Michael later that same afternoon.

She answered the phone on the first ring. "Percival School, Brittany Evans speaking."

"Is Brittany Evans thinking about me as much as I'm thinking about her?" Michael asked.

Brittany murmured her answer into the receiver. "More."

"You want more?" His voice was a velvety drawl. "Lady, I can hardly lift my pen as it is."

"I meant I'm missing you even more," she retorted.

"Impossible. I think you've put a spell on me."

"I was just about to accuse you of the same thing," she told him with a husky laugh.

"I haven't been able to get much work done today at all. How about you?"

"Same here. I don't seem to be able to concentrate properly. And the kids could sense that. They were a real handful today. Of course, Tiffany told everyone about seeing us together on Saturday."

"What was the reaction?" Michael asked.

"The kids miss you. They'd like to see you again."

"How about if I drop by tomorrow morning?" he suggested.

"That would be great!"

"Fine." He paused before adding, "I'm not sure I could find my way to the school again after all this time, though. So it might be a good idea for me to spend the night at your place and follow you in to work tomorrow morning."

"Sounds like a good idea to me," she agreed.

The children greeted Michael with enthusiasm Tuesday morning. Brittany had greeted him with even more enthusiasm in the privacy of her apartment the night before.

"Mr. Devlin, Clarissa wants to say hi!" Maria exclaimed.

Michael dutifully bent to greet the doll. "Hi, Clarissa. I hope your baby carriage has been working okay?"

"It's okey-dokey," Maria answered with a beaming smile.

"It sure is," Michael repeated, watching Brittany's face with an intensity that told her he was remembering the loving they'd shared last night.

Marcia and Joan shared a knowing grin as they viewed that look. Even Bud noticed the electricity flowing between Brittany and Michael.

"It looks like your plan worked," Bud told Arlene over dinner later that night.

Arlene sighed wistfully. "I wish I could have seen them together. You know, I haven't even met Brittany Evans yet and that hardly seems fair after all the work we went through to get those two together."

Bud just smiled at his wife's complaining voice. "Go on. You loved every minute of it."

Arlene smiled in agreement. "You're right. I'm just a romantic at heart, I guess. You think they're going to make it as a couple?"

"Only time will tell. One thing's for sure, we've made it as a couple. What d'ya say we put on a Benny Goodman record and jitterbug tonight. Let the young folks worry about themselves."

Brittany didn't have cause to worry until Sunday. Michael was taking her out for Sunday brunch, but he wasn't telling her where. Not that that was unusual for him, she reassured herself. Michael loved surprising her.

Since it was raining, Michael was driving the Firebird and Brittany's hand rested beneath his on the steering wheel. "Come on, give me a hint," she tried coaxing him. "We're going north, right?"

"You've been peeking at the compass again." He shook his head at her and said, "Shame on you."

The closer they got to Baltimore, the more uneasy Brittany became. She tried ignoring her ominous premonition. Surely Michael wouldn't . . . he couldn't . . . but he was.

"We're eating at my folks' house." He made the cheerful announcement now that it was too late for Brittany to do anything about it. "I want you to meet them."

"Michael, you can't just take me there uninvited."

"You were invited."

She snatched her hand away from his. "Well, I didn't accept the invitation." She became more flustered with each passing block. "I didn't even know about any invitation. Why didn't you tell me?"

"I didn't want you getting nervous about

it," he explained in a tone of voice meant to soothe her.

It didn't work. "I am nervous. I'm not ready for this. I'm not dressed for this." She ran an agitated hand over her blue silk dress. The outfit was fine for a nice restaurant, but too splashy for a family get-together.

"It's too late now." He pulled the car to a stop in front of a brick row house. "We're here."

There were already several cars parked in the driveway so Michael parked the Firebird on the street. The neighborhood had seen better days. The houses were built smack against each other with only a few feet separating them.

Short of throwing a temper tantrum in the car, there was little Brittany could do but get out when Michael opened the car door for her. Swallowing her panic, she allowed him to take her around the side of the house to the back door.

They entered the kitchen where several women were seated around a Formica table while a group of children ran wild, screaming and shouting at the tops of their lungs.

"Look, Michael's here!" one of the women shouted above the bedlam.

All the women got up and descended en masse to hug Michael.

"So this is your girl, huh?" someone said.

Now all eyes turned to Brittany.

"Brittany, this is my mom." He hugged the ample woman at his side before pointing to the other women. "And that's Aunt Meg, my sister Peg, sister-in-law Linda, cousin Mary, and sister Sue. Everybody — this is Brittany Evans."

Brittany shook Mrs. Devlin's hand and smiled at the other women, frantically trying to remember whether the redhead was cousin Mary or sister Sue.

"I'm glad to meet you, Mrs. Devlin," Brittany said in a polite voice.

"Don't be so formal," Mrs. Devlin scolded. "Call me Carolyn."

The kids ran through the kitchen again before exiting down a long hallway.

Brittany was urged over to the kitchen table where she was offered coffee and cookies. Somehow in the transition from back door to kitchen table, she'd lost Michael.

Catching sight of the sudden desperation in Brittany's eyes, Carolyn patted her hand and said, "Don't worry about Michael. The men are all watching baseball in the front room. That's where he'll be."

He'd left her! Under normal circumstances Brittany wouldn't have been bothered. But these weren't normal circumstances for her. The mob rule going on in the kitchen was too reminiscent of scenes from her own past

— scenes she'd rather forget.

"So, Brittany, Michael tells us you're a teacher?"

The question startled her. Brittany thought it had come from Peg, but it was hard to tell because several people were all talking at once. "That's right." Could they tell how ill at ease she felt? How out of place?

The herd of kids, aged four to twelve, stampeded through the kitchen again as Peg leaned across the Formica table to say, "The kindergarten teacher my kid's got is awful. Mrs. Bloom is her name."

"Mrs. Bloom?" Brittany repeated, trying to hold back the wave of bad memories being revived by this domestic uproar. "*The* Mrs. Bloom?"

"The one and only," Peg confirmed. "She's been teaching for practically half a century now."

Brittany jumped in her seat when Aunt Meg, who was sitting beside her, suddenly yelled, "You worry too much about little Joey!"

"You'd worry, too, if your grandkids went to a public school," Peg retorted.

"Your Uncle Rob has worked night and day at his construction company to make the money we've got!" Aunt Meg continued in the same strident, ear-splitting voice that had earned her the family nickname of "the Screamer." "Maybe if your husband wasn't

187

such a dreamer, he'd be able to send his kids to a decent school!"

Peg got up and left the kitchen in a huff.

Her seat was immediately taken by a teenage girl. "Hi, I'm Ellen, Michael's youngest sister. You must be Brittany."

Brittany nodded and attempted a smile. The muscles in her throat were taut from stress and she couldn't manage to speak. Aunt Meg's voice had sounded all too familiar.

"How're you holding up?" Ellen asked while applying a final coat of nail polish.

Brittany shot Ellen a startled look. Was she that transparent? Could everyone see the panic churning within her?

"These family dos are always a drag. You need a scorecard to keep track." A car beeped outside and Ellen twisted the cap back on the bottle of blood-red nail polish. "Oops, there's my date. Gotta go!"

"Ellen, you tell that boy to come to the door to pick you up next time," Carolyn Devlin ordered.

"I will, Mom."

"And you be back home by ten."

"Aw, Mom . . ."

"Those are the rules. You broke curfew last week, you're lucky your father didn't ground you."

Ellen made a face and walked out the back door.

"She's seventeen," Carolyn turned to tell Brittany after Ellen had left. "She's our youngest and probably our wildest."

"You spoil her!" Aunt Meg yelled.

Carolyn nodded with a smile. "She's my baby."

Brittany didn't get a chance to meet Michael's brothers until it was time to sit down and eat. Instead of being invited into the dining room, Brittany was handed a bowl of salad and told to go downstairs. There, in a semifinished basement, was a long table already set up with more place settings than Brittany could count. The women were busy bustling around the table and relaying the food down the long flight of stairs.

Suddenly, as if on call, the men came downstairs — now that there was no more work to be done. There were a dozen of them, all arguing about some player in the Baltimore Orioles.

"Hey, little brother, is this your lady?" one of them asked.

Michael nodded from his position across the room, where it looked as if he were penned in by a pair of quarterbacks. "Yeah. Brittany, that's my older brother Joe. And these two guys are brother-in-laws Rick and Steve."

Joe smiled at her and went on arguing about the baseball game. Rick and Steve didn't even perform that small courtesy.

Brittany didn't get any opportunity to speak to Michael during the meal. In fact, there was little opportunity to hold any kind of civilized conversation. Instead, a free-for-all, no-holds-barred verbal battle seemed to go on with everyone vying for attention: the adults, the kids, the two dogs. A much younger Brittany had seen and heard it all before. She really didn't want to live through it again.

By the time the meal was over, and the men disappeared again, Brittany was on the ragged edge. Her hands shook as she helped clear the table, and the throbbing in her temples warned of an impending migraine. She longed for some peace and quiet.

It took her another half hour to make her escape from the kitchen. The memories were overwhelming her. She had to find Michael and leave. Skirting the kids fighting in the hallway, she finally found Michael sitting in the living room, straddling a straight-backed chair, seemingly intent on the baseball game being televised. None of the men noticed her hovering in the doorway.

"I can't believe that last call," one of the men was grousing.

"I can't believe Michael's actually brought a girl home." Joe reached over to sock

Michael's arm. "This is the guy who claims he likes his steak rare and his women bare!"

As if sensing her presence Michael looked toward the doorway and saw Brittany standing there, her face pale, her eyes remote. Cursing his older brother's loose tongue, Michael stood up and quickly joined Brittany.

"Ignore Joe, he's an idiot," Michael said in a rueful undertone.

Brittany wasn't upset by Joe's comment. She already knew far too well about the gulf in life-styles separating her from Michael and his family. "I've got a headache, do you mind if we leave now?"

They were out of the house within minutes. Brittany was quiet all during the ride back to Annapolis. Michael began to wish he'd handled the situation differently. Dropping Brittany in the midst of his family may not have been the best way to introduce her to them. But breaking with tradition and staying with Brittany in the kitchen or bringing her with him to the front room would only have drawn more attention to her and made it even harder on her.

Michael loved his family, but they were a rowdy bunch. Even he could take them only in small doses. He could imagine how they must seem to an outsider.

He shot her a worried glance, wishing she'd talk to him, tell him what to do to make her feel better. At first he'd thought she'd been upset about Joe's asinine comment, but something told him that Brittany's distress went much deeper than that.

She finally spoke when he pulled into the parking lot in front of her apartment building. "I'd rather you didn't come in tonight."

"Is your headache worse?" he asked with quiet concern.

Brittany nodded.

Michael couldn't leave things as they were. He had to say something by way of explanation. "Look, I know my family is a bit wild . . ."

She interrupted him, her voice tense. "Our backgrounds are quite different."

Even though he'd expected her to say those words, actually hearing them dealt a serious blow to his pride. Anger rose within him. "I'm not good enough for you, is that what you're saying? An Ivy Leaguer is more your type?"

"I don't want to talk about this now. I really don't feel well." Brittany wasn't lying. The emotional turmoil she'd been through had indeed left her feeling ill. She couldn't face a scene with Michael now.

"When will we talk? Tomorrow?"

"I've got parents conferences all next week, Michael."

"Then when will you see me again?" he demanded in a taut voice, but it was only a formality. He knew what was coming.

"I don't know," She turned away from him. "I think we both need time to think."

Her polite rejection hit Michael with the force of a physical blow. He wanted to rant and rave; he wanted to slam his fist into something solid. But such displays of emotion weren't his way. The only sign he gave of his pain was in the stiffening of his shoulders and the curtness of his voice as he said, "Fine. Maybe it would be best if you did some thinking, and finally made up your mind what it is you want. Because I already know that I sure as hell don't want a woman who doesn't want me."

Brittany didn't say a word in rebuttal.

Her cool remoteness spurred Michael into leaning across her to shove open the passenger door with deliberate disrespect. "I've had it with chasing you, Brittany Evans. The party's over. Go find some other jerk to lead around by the nose!"

As Brittany got out of the car she spoke with regal dignity. "I'm sorry."

Once she'd left, Michael closed his eyes and whispered, "So am I, Brittany Evans. So am I."

CHAPTER TEN

As soon as she entered her apartment Brittany headed directly for the protected confines of her balcony. She sat outside despite the fact that a misty rain was now falling over Chesapeake Bay. The overhanging roof protected her from the rain, but nothing could protect her from the painful memories.

Brittany knew the story by heart, for it involved her own parents. Her father had been a bartender who'd worked at a party being given by her mother's wealthy parents. Her mother, a popular debutante, had been swept off her feet by the dashing bartender and she'd eloped with him a week later. Ten months after that Brittany was born.

Brittany's earliest memories were of the conflicts between her father's way of life and her mother's. She could still remember going over to her paternal grandparents' house as a little girl and being frightened by all the screaming and yelling. The older children had mocked her fears and taunted her. The domestic chaos at the Devlins' home had been too reminiscent of those scary childhood memories. In fact one reason Michael's Aunt Meg had upset Brittany so much was that the woman had sounded just like her father's mother; both had voices that were coarsely strident.

At the other end of the cultural spectrum were her mother's parents. While not thrilled with their daughter's choice of husband, they never voiced their disapproval or made it felt in any way. Brittany had always loved going over to their house and listening to her grandma play the grand piano that stood in the music room.

The situation between Brittany's parents worsened until her father took off when she was eight. Brittany had neither seen nor heard from either her father or his family since then. *And the moral of the story?* she asked herself as she watched the gradual darkening of the sky. *Stick with your own kind, someone who shares the same interests as you do, the same background.* It was a philosophy she'd strictly adhered to until meeting Michael.

Michael. She'd let her love for him blind her to her own limitations. She simply couldn't handle the differences between them. Love wasn't always enough. Her own parents' experience proved that. They had loved each other in the beginning; her mother had told her as much. Her mother had also told her that coming from such diverse worlds had been the main reason the marriage had failed. A case of culture shock, plain and simple. And that was why, in the interest of self-preservation, Brittany felt compelled to step away from Michael while she still had the strength to do so.

The tears rolled down her face, leaving a streaky path in their wake. And once she started crying, she didn't seem to be able to stop. The bouts of weeping recurred throughout the night and left her feeling completely drained the next morning.

She wasn't the type who was able to cry daintily; her blotchy face and swollen eyes affirmed that. When no amount of makeup was able to disguise the fact that she'd been crying, Brittany wearily decided to call in sick. Since the children's activities had already been planned ahead of time, Joan and Marcia would be able to cover for her.

The news that Brittany was ill was accepted by everyone at the school — with the exception of Bud, who had a funny feeling something was wrong. As a result of his involvement in Operation Cupid, Bud couldn't help but feel somewhat responsible toward Brittany, so he acted on his hunch and gave Arlene a quick call during his lunch break.

"Security Management Systems."

Bud got right to the point. "Arlene, it's me. Brittany Evans didn't come in to work today. She phoned in sick. Has Michael said anything about her being ill?"

"No, he hasn't said anything, but then he just arrived himself." It was almost twelve-fifteen. "He didn't look too healthy either. You don't think they've fought again, do you?"

Bud was already having second thoughts. "It really isn't any of our business. . . ."

"I'll check it out and get back to you," Arlene said in a brisk voice that indicated that her boss was suddenly within hearing distance. "Good-bye."

Arlene didn't know how to describe Michael's mood. His glacial manner was meant to keep everyone at bay and it was very effective. Even Arlene was discouraged from asking the questions gathering at the tip of her tongue. Instead she made the mild observation, "I've seen you look better, boss." She handed him his phone messages. "There must be something going around, apparently Brittany didn't show up for work today either."

Michael didn't even acknowledge that he'd heard Arlene's comment about Brittany. He simply ordered her to bring her steno pad into his office. When she did so he proceeded to launch into a long and detailed dictation for a bid, a bid that had to be sent out immediately. The way in which he delivered that final order told Arlene that this was no time to push her luck.

As Arlene left to type out six copies of the multi-page bid she was wishing for a hi-tech word processor instead of her work-horse electric typewriter.

Michael's wish was more complicated than that. He wished he could forget Brittany; he wished he'd never taken her to meet his family; never gotten involved with her; never gone to the Percival School in the first place! Women! Michael picked up a file describing an assignment that would involve some out-of-state travel. He'd been considering delegating the job to someone else, but now he decided that getting out of town might be just the thing he needed.

Michael was already out of state by the time Brittany returned to work Tuesday morning. She could hide her feelings from her co-workers, but the children sensed something was wrong.

After Brittany finished reading a story, Maria walked up to her and climbed onto Brittany's lap for a cuddle. "You're sad," Maria said with a knowing nod. "Me too. I don't wanna leave here and go to some other school. I'll miss you!" She threw her arms around Brittany's neck.

"I'll miss you too," Brittany murmured, swallowing back tears. *You'd think you'd have cried yourself dry by now,* she chastised herself.

"Is that why you're sad?" Maria asked her. Brittany nodded.

Bud and Arlene watched the goings-on with confusion and distress. "What could have gone wrong?" Arlene asked her husband for the umpteenth time. She and Bud were in their living room.

Bud's thatch of silver-gray hair was all that could be seen above the evening newspaper as he replied, "I don't know, but this time I think we should definitely stay out of it. They're adults, it's about time they learned how to deal with their own lives."

"I realize that." Arlene looked up from the afghan she was knitting. "But the way they're dealing with it is all wrong."

"Then they'll have to learn from their mistakes."

The phone woke Brittany on Saturday morning. She'd spent another sleepless night, tossing and turning until dawn, unable to turn off the thoughts running through her mind. She reached for the phone and mumbled a fuzzy "Hello?" into the receiver.

"Britt, dear, it's me — Mother," a cheerful feminine voice announced with a hint of an English accent. "I don't have much time to talk. Stuart had to fly to Washington on a sudden business trip and he invited me to come along."

Smothering a sleepy yawn, Brittany said, "Wonderful, Mother. When will you be coming to Washington?"

"We're here already, dear. We flew in on the Concorde today."

Brittany's eyes flew open and sought out her bedside digital clock. It was 11:55 in the morning! She'd never slept that late before.

"I've rented a car and thought I'd drive up to see you while Stuart is busy with his meetings this afternoon. So I'll see you in about an hour, dear. Cheerio."

A second later Brittany heard the dial tone. She hung up the phone and sank back onto her bed with a groan. An hour! She had only one hour to get ready? Her mother's eagle eye was sure to discern the signs of strain on her only daughter's face.

Brittany kicked back the bedcovers and raced into the bathroom, intent on waking herself up with a shower. Her hair and body were squeaky clean in record time. She was still drying herself with a towel as she rifled through her closet in search of some flashy ensemble that might divert her mother's attention from the thinness of her face to the voguishness of her outfit.

Ah, the dark plum tailored trousers and

the brilliant yellow blouse would do nicely. Only after she'd donned both articles of clothing did Brittany remember that Daniel had told her she looked like a lemon and grape ice-cream cone the last time she'd worn the outfit. Too bad. It was too late to change. And at least she wasn't *shaped* like an ice-cream cone. In fact she'd lost weight because her appetite had all but disappeared since she'd broken off with Michael.

Michael. There he was, in her thoughts again. Dashing into her living room, Brittany tried venting her frustration by thoroughly vacuuming every nook and cranny in her apartment. She even went so far as to put on the attachments and vacuum the windowsills and the furniture upholstery — even the leaves of her avocado tree! But her thoughts kept drifting back to Michael.

The doorbell rang just as Brittany stashed the vacuum back in the closet. She ran one final appraising glance around her now spotless living room while running a smoothing hand through her short hair. Then she put a smile on her face and pulled open the front door

"Mother!" Brittany exclaimed, hugging her warmly.

Despite Brittany's preparations, her mother knew something was wrong the minute she set eyes on her daughter. "What have you been doing to yourself?" Charlene

Evans asked with maternal horror as soon as she stepped inside.

Brittany closed the door and did a small pirouette. "You don't like my haircut?" Her mother hadn't seen the new style before.

"The haircut is too short but that's not what I'm talking about. I'm talking about that look."

"What look?"

Charlene gave a reprimanding tap to her daughter's chin. "This haunted look."

"I always look like this by the end of the school year," Brittany said in a flippant voice. "That's why they give teachers the entire summer off, so we can recover. But let's not stand here chatting." Brittany cast an arm around her mother's shoulders and ushered her into the living room. As well as having the same hair color, mother and daughter were practically the same height. "Come on in and sit down. Tell me about your flight. I like your suit. Did you get it in Paris? And those shoes! Are they lizard skin?"

Charlene allowed herself to be led over to the couch but the moment she sat down she resumed her interrogation. "Brittany, I'm your mother. I know when you're evading a question. Now tell me what's wrong. Is it a man?"

Seeing the determined expression on her mother's face, Brittany realized that she wasn't about to let go of the subject. "Yes, it's a man."

"What happened?" Charlene asked in a calm voice.

Brittany got to her feet and began pacing. "Really, you'd think I'd know better, especially after having seen what you and my father went through."

Charlene looked surprised. "You haven't mentioned your father in years."

"I haven't thought about him in years, either. Then something happened to make it all come back to me."

"Here." Charlene patted the couch cushion. "You sit down, and I'll make us both some tea and we'll talk about it."

Brittany waved her mother back into her seat. "I'll get the tea, Mom. You sit down. You're probably exhausted from the trip."

"Really, the Concorde made the trip much easier. That's why Stuart always flies supersonic whenever he can."

From the kitchen Brittany asked, "How is Stuart?"

"Fine." Charlene raised her voice so Brittany could hear her. "He wanted to stop by and see you but he's got a meeting in Washington this afternoon. He sends his love and says to save tomorrow night for dinner. He's inviting you to the best restaurant in the capital."

"I can hardly wait." Stuart Evans had

married Brittany's mother when Brittany was ten. He'd adopted Brittany and assumed the role of her father with a proficiency he'd already displayed in his role of executive-vice president of one of the Fortune Five Hundred corporations. Last year he'd been promoted to oversee operations in England and Europe.

With a potful of tea between them Charlene finally said, "Okay, now tell me what's been going on."

In between sips Brittany gave her mother a condensed version of her relationship with Michael.

"So you're telling me that you broke up with this Michael because you both come from different worlds?" Charlene asked.

"My reasons had nothing to do with snobbish prejudices, Mother," Brittany retorted, stung by her mother's perplexity. "You of all people should know that. But a relationship between two people needs a common ground to grow on."

"It sounds like you didn't begin worrying about the lack of common ground until you met his family," Charlene noted astutely.

"That's right," Brittany agreed with a sigh. "That's when it really hit me."

"Oh, dear." Charlene set down her teacup. "I fear this may be all my fault."

Brittany looked at her mother in surprise. "What makes you say that?"

"You see yourself making the same mistake with Michael as I made with your father, right?"

Brittany nodded.

"And you think you can't make a go of things together because of your differing backgrounds?"

Again Brittany nodded.

"Then it is my fault." Charlene smoothed back a wisp of hair from an otherwise perfectly coiffured hairdo. "When you were younger it seemed simpler to blame your father's disappearance on the differences between his world and mine. My reasons weren't altogether selfless, it was easier on me too. On my pride. But I see now that I've burdened you with a misconception." Taking a deep breath, as if for courage, Charlene said, "Brittany, the problem wasn't caused by your father's blue-collar background. I've learned since then that many of my high-society friends have had the same problem. The truth is, your father was a compulsive gambler. He went through my inheritance money in the nine years we were together. When the money ran out, so did he."

It took Brittany a moment to comprehend what her mother was telling her. "Why didn't you ever mention this before?"

Charlene's expression was regretful. "As I said, my pride. I hated admitting that I had been foolish enough to allow him access to all my money. Somehow it was easier to blame things on a broader issue like class differences than tell a little girl her father had left because betting on the horses was more important to him than his family was."

"But surely the social differences between you had some part in the breakup of the marriage?" Brittany asked in a shaken voice.

Charlene shook her head. "The unbridgeable differences between your father and I were caused by his gambling. Had he not been addicted to that, I'm sure we could have overcome the other problems. Your father was a gambler — that's the kind of man he was, first and foremost. And that's what you want to look for in a man, what he is first and foremost. Not what lies on the surface, but what's underneath it all. Keeping that in mind, are you and Michael so different after all?"

Brittany searched her heart and found the answer. She'd made a terrible mistake. "What do I do now?" She unintentionally murmured the question aloud.

"You know I'm not the kind of mother to interfere," Charlene retorted with a grin. "But if I were, I'd say if you want the man — go after him!"

CHAPTER ELEVEN

He's not coming, Brittany thought to herself with fatalistic resignation as she studied the people gathered at the Percival School's end-of-the-year party.

The idea had seemed so brilliant when she'd first devised it. A huge handwritten personalized invitation from every member of Brittany's class, and most of the members of everyone else's class as well, had been made out and sent to Michael. Brittany knew Michael had received the special invitation; she'd asked Bud to check with Arlene to verify its arrival.

Maybe I should have put RSVP on the bottom of it, she thought to herself as she nibbled nervously at her fingernails. *But If I had, Michael might well have refused.* At least this way she could hope for a while longer. After all, the party was only just getting started; people were still arriving.

A sticky little hand tugging on Brittany's washable black skirt caught her attention.

"Can't I come back next year?" Carrie asked Brittany. "If I promise to be good and eat all my vegetables?"

Brittany stooped down so that she could speak to Carrie face-to-face. After putting an encouraging arm around the little girl's shoulders, Brittany said, "You're going to be going to a lovely school next year. The same school Matthew and Adam and Daniel are going to." Most, but not all, of the children did end up going on to Brentwood Academy. Some would be moving out of the area altogether, like Tiffany, whose mother planned on moving to San Francisco for a reconciliation with her former husband.

Carrie leaned closer to ask, "Don't any girls go there?"

"Sure they do," Brittany replied. "Maria will probably go there too."

Carrie thought about that a minute. "How do you know I'll like it?"

"Because I know the teacher you'll have and she's real nice." Brittany's voice lowered as if she were sharing a secret with Carrie. "In fact, she's coming to our party today."

Carrie's face brightened. "She is?"

Brittany nodded. "And she's looking forward to meeting you." Inviting Brentwood's first-grade teachers had been Brittany's idea. The exchange program had been in effect two years now and made the transition from the Percival School to a larger private school easier on the children.

Carrie smiled and skipped away, reassured by Brittany's words. Watching Carrie go, Brittany experienced a funny tug at her heart, the same tug she felt at the end of each school year. The children had grown so much since they'd started in her class ten months ago. Grown not only in inches, but in maturity as well. Their attention span was longer, their artwork was more interesting, and their storytelling showed more creativity. It was rewarding for Brittany to see the signs of change and to know she'd had an influence in their lives.

Michael had had an even larger influence on her own life. Since she'd talked with her mother last week Brittany had picked up the phone a hundred times to call him. But what she had to say to him couldn't be said over the telephone. It had to be said in person. Which was why she'd thought this party would be the best chance she'd have. And when Maria had suggested Michael attend the party, Brittany had wholeheartedly agreed.

But all her plans seemed to have been in vain, because so far there was no sign of Michael and the party had officially started almost half an hour ago now. As Brittany circulated among the parents and students she kept a sharp lookout for a man with massive shoulders and sun-streaked brown hair. Eventually Matthew's parents snared her in a lengthy conversation about their son's development.

"I agree," Brittany said when she was finally given an opportunity to speak. "It was very innovative of Matthew to bring in that graph from *Scientific American* for our last Show and Tell."

Matthew's father preened.

"However," Brittany continued, "I was equally pleased to see Matthew's growth in creativity over the past year. He composed a wonderful story during our storytelling hour, you know. He really seemed to blossom when his story was chosen by the other students as the one they'd enjoyed playacting in the most." The story, about a family of lion cubs who'd lost their parents in the woods, had been full of action and adventure. "I hope you'll continue to work with him to expand his imagination and encourage his curiosity."

When Matthew's father launched into a lengthy dissertation about science and curiosity, Brittany allowed her eyes to again circumnavigate the classroom. Her searching gaze located one man out in the front foyer who looked familiar. Richard Covington. What was he doing here? Had she invited him earlier in the year and forgotten about it?

Brittany made her excuses to Matthew's parents and was about to approach Richard when she saw Shelly waltz up to him and give him a hearty kiss. When the couple caught sight of Brittany their faces became sheepish. Shelly spoke a few words to Richard and then hurried over to speak with Brittany.

"I didn't realize you two knew each other," Brittany said.

"We met at the Spring Festival," Shelly replied with a nervous smile. "Richard told me that you two had only been seeing each other casually, nothing serious. You don't mind, do you?"

"Not at all." Brittany's smile was genuine. "I wish you both all the best."

"Thanks." Shelly hugged Brittany. "I wish you all the best with Michael too. I never had a chance with him, you know. You were the one he wanted all along."

As if Shelly had recited some magic incantation, Michael suddenly appeared in the doorway.

Brittany drank in the sight of him. The dark slacks he wore made him look leaner while the white cotton of his short-sleeved shirt was a stunning contrast to his golden tan. Her hopeful pleasure dimmed somewhat when she noted the starkness of his profile and the remoteness of his eyes. He looked so unapproachable that she actually shivered.

Then Maria spotted Michael and ran up

to greet him. "You came! You came!"

As soon as Michael caught sight of the little girl, he smiled. His face lost its sternness, and the ice in his green eyes melted. "Hi, Maria. How are you?"

"Okey-dokey and Clarissa's okey-dokey too!"

How Brittany hoped that Michael would smile at her again soon. Would he understand when she explained herself to him? He had to. She'd simply keep on explaining until he did.

As she approached Michael, Brittany's heart pounded beneath her turquoise blouse. The closer she came to him, the faster her heartbeat became. Her palms were damp and her fingers icy by the time she reached him.

"I'm glad you could come," she whispered in a husky voice.

"I came to see the kids." Not to see you. The words may have been unspoken but they were clearly received, nonetheless.

Although she expected resistance, Brittany still quivered from his hurtful greeting.

As if to emphasize that Brittany was the only one being singled out for such distant behavior, Michael smiled at Maria. "Maria here wants me to meet her parents." When he looked at Brittany again, his eyes turned cold. So did his voice. "Excuse us."

It was tough but Brittany weathered the

encounter. The hardest part was watching him walk away from her. And yet that was what she'd done to him.

The realization stiffened her backbone. She wouldn't give up. But Michael was equally determined. Each time she approached him, Michael made it a point to excuse himself on some pretext or another.

When he saw that Brittany wasn't put off by his avoidance of her, Michael began anticipating her moves and sabotaging them by wandering from one group of people to another, always staying one step ahead of her. Although Brittany was an expert at this kind of social hopscotch, having honed her skills at numerous social functions, she still couldn't catch up with him.

As time went on Brittany became increasingly frustrated. She had to speak to Michael alone, yet how could she when he avoided her like the plague?

Brittany was still mulling over a possible answer to that question even as she thanked Daniel's parents for the donation check they'd just handed her.

"You want to be sure and put that in a safe place, now," Daniel's father told her in a teasing voice.

Brittany smiled. "If you'll excuse me a moment, I'll go do just that."

She welcomed the chance to get away for

a while. Perhaps with a few moments of quiet thought she could come up with some sort of plan. Her fingers absently twirled the combination knob of her office safe as her mind struggled for inspiration.

Impatience made her pull open the safe's metal door with more than usual force. The move dislodged a pile of important school records. "Damn!" She grabbed the papers before they slid out and shoved them back inside. As she did so her fingers encountered cool, hard metal. "Ouch!"

At first Brittany thought she must have rammed her knuckles against Bud's gun. "That's a good way to shoot yourself," she muttered, gazing into the safe with extreme caution. But upon closer inspection she found that Bud's gun was on the opposite end of the safe. "So what did I hit?" She carefully moved some papers aside and found an old pair of open handcuffs, a forgotten possession of Sam's.

As Brittany pulled the handcuffs from the safe a wild idea was already forming in her head. Desperate times call for desperate measures. Wasn't that a famous quote? If not, it should be. If all else failed, here was one way to keep Michael in place long enough to talk to him.

Wait just a minute, she silently ordered her wayward thoughts. *Are you seriously considering handcuffing the man you love?*

She set the handcuffs on her desk before shaking her head at them. "This is too wild," she said, as if verbalizing the words would stop her from doing something foolish. Besides, how would she manage it?

Well, first she'd have to get him into the office. That shouldn't be too hard. A phone call, yes, that would work. She could tell Michael he had a phone call.

No, she couldn't. She couldn't get close enough to him to tell him anything. Besides, in the mood Michael was in, he probably wouldn't believe her. It was too obvious.

All right then, someone else would have to tell him there was a phone call. Who? Her eyes alighted on the gun still visible in the open safe. Bud! Perfect!

In her eagerness to get the ball rolling, Brittany almost forgot to put the donation check she'd just received into the safe. Tossing it inside, she hurriedly shut the safe door. Then she hid the incriminating handcuffs beneath some loose papers on her desk, so that they were hidden from sight but still easily accessible.

The moment Brittany stepped out of her office she was cornered by Marcia. "The children are getting antsy, if you'll excuse the expression. I think it's time we did the musical presentation."

"The musical presentation?" Brittany was

forced to shift mental gears in a hurry. "Oh, right, the musical presentation. Now?"

"I think we should do it now, before they become impossible," Marcia said.

Brittany sighed. Her personal plans would have to wait a few minutes. "Okay. Break out the tambourines."

The children had made the tambourines themselves, constructing them out of paper plates either taped or glued together with jelly beans inside. Close supervision over the project had ensured that most of the jelly beans had ended up in the tambourines and not in the children's stomachs.

The children were all gathered up and grouped together in Shelly's classroom. Parents were shooed out with instructions to wait in Brittany's classroom until the performance began.

Brittany clapped her hands to get everyone's attention. "Okay, now. Let's practice the song we're going to sing."

Brittany went through the motions of the song "I'm a Little Teapot" with the children. She ended up with one hand on her hip and the other held out like a spout as she bent over sideways in the final verse: "Tip me over and pour me out!"

"Very good," she congratulated them. "Just remember that all the teapots should lean over toward the windows in the end and that way you won't bump into each other, okay?"

"I'm not a teapot, I'm an espresso machine," Tiffany announced.

"You're weird," Kevin declared.

Maria immediately came to Tiffany's defense. "She is not."

"She is too."

"Is not!"

"Is too!"

"Msss Evans, when do we get to eat the jelly beans?" Daniel asked, more concerned about the candy than the debate raging between Maria and Kevin.

"These are super jelly beans," Adam was telling one of Shelly's students. "They'll turn you into Superman if you eat them."

Brittany was tempted to turn them all into dinosaurs if they didn't behave. "No one eats the jelly beans until after the song. Now, where's the rest of the tambourine section?" The children were supposed to be divided into two groups, one acting as teapots, the other singing and playing homemade tambourines.

When all the children were finally in their proper positions, the door to Shelly's classroom was opened and the parents invited to come stand inside — there wasn't room for anyone to be seated — and listen to a musical extravaganza. With the exception of Tiffany's espresso-machine routine, the performance went off without a hitch. The children grinned at the hearty applause they were given by the standing-room-only audience.

As the enthusiastic clapping died away Brittany came to the foreground to make an announcement. "We've got a special selection of goodies in the kitchen, international delicacies from Japan, Great Britain, Spain, and Egypt to give you a taste of the different cultures of some of our students. And we've got chairs set outside so you can enjoy the refreshments out in the sun."

As the crowd quickly began to head off toward the kitchen, Brittany spotted Michael deep in conversation with Adam's father. Good, he would be kept busy for a while. She paused in front of her office to look for Bud, and grabbed his arm as he went past her on his way to the kitchen.

"Bud, would you do me a favor?"

"Sure. What's up?"

"I need you to tell Michael that there's a phone call for him. He can pick it up in my office."

"Why don't you tell him?"

"I would if I could get him to stand in one place long enough," Brittany retorted.

Bud had also noticed Michael's diversionary tactics. "Okay, I'll tell him."

"Thanks."

The moment Bud turned away, Brittany

slipped back into her office. She took the phone receiver off the hook and left it sitting in the middle of her desk, well away from the corner where she'd hidden the open handcuffs.

Everything was set up, now all she needed was Michael. Perhaps she wouldn't have to utilize her final plan after all; perhaps he'd listen to her without forcing her to resort to dramatic means. As she nervously waited near the file cabinet she certainly hoped that would be the case. Handcuffing one hundred and eighty pounds of angry man was not her idea of a good time!

The office door opened and Michael walked in. He paused the moment he saw Brittany. "Bud told me there was a call for me."

Brittany swallowed the lump in her throat and nodded toward the phone. As soon as Michael moved forward she closed the door behind him.

By this time Michael had reached the receiver and realized there was only a dial tone.

He fixed her with a narrow-eyed stare and spoke in a voice guaranteed to instill fear at fifty paces. "There never was any phone call, was there?" He hung up the receiver with dangerous restraint. "It was a setup."

"I needed to . . ." Was that high-pitched soprano voice hers? Brittany cleared her throat and started again. "I needed to talk to you." There, that sounded better.

"We don't have anything to say."

"*I* have something to say."

"I don't want to hear it."

Why did he have to be so stubborn? "Michael, I have to explain —"

"Spare me the hearts-and-flowers routine," he ordered in a harsh voice.

Brittany saw him turning to leave and knew what she had to do. In her mind's eye she saw a flashback of the annual school field trip to the local police station where the officers had shown the children how handcuffs worked. Brittany had watched the routine for several years running now, never suspecting that one day she'd be reaching for a pair of handcuffs herself and thinking, *This is it — go for it!*

Michael didn't expect Brittany to grab him by the arm in an attempt to detain him.

She made the most of his brief pause by slapping one cuff around his right wrist before closing the other cuff around her own left wrist.

"What the hell . . . ?" Michael looked down in astonished disbelief at the circlet of metal connecting his wrist to hers.

"I'm not letting you go," she stated with a courage which was in dire need of bolstering.

"What do you think you're doing?" Mi-

220

chael asked in a voice he thought was very calm given the circumstances.

"I'm making sure you stay here and listen to me." Anger lent her strength. "I tried everything else, but *noooo,* you wouldn't listen! So I had to use these handcuffs as a last resort."

Holding up his shackled wrist, Michael drawled, "Handcuffing me is not the way to endear yourself to me."

"I'm not trying to endear myself," she retorted. "I'm trying to explain myself. Will you listen to me now?"

Michael studied her face for a moment. There was no mistaking the fire of determination in her blue eyes. Hell, he had to give her credit. She certainly had guts. "I don't suppose I have a choice."

Brittany sagged back against her desk in relief. Her unguarded movement jerked Michael toward her, forcing him to put out his hands to prevent a collision. His warm fingers circled her bare arms, forming a chain even more binding than the metal handcuffs. Brittany's lips parted to accommodate her quickened breathing. It had been so long since she'd felt his touch, a sense of expectancy washed over her with mercurial swiftness.

Looking into his eyes, Brittany became entangled in their misty green depths. The mask melted as the icy impassiveness of his expression was thawed by the gradual dawning of passion. She noted the conflict in his gaze as he stared down at her with fierce intensity.

Gathering his thoughts, Michael stepped away from her. "What was it you wanted to tell me?" Now that he was no longer touching her, the smoke screen was back in place.

Despite his withdrawal, Brittany was still encouraged by her brief glimpse of the man behind the mask. "I wanted to explain why I broke things off and to try and make amends if I can."

"I already know why you broke it off. You made it pretty obvious. We come from different worlds," Michael stated without emotion.

"You come from Baltimore and I come from Annapolis," Brittany replied with a wistful smile. "The two really aren't that far apart."

"You didn't think so when I took you to visit my family."

Her smile died as she looked down at the metal temporarily linking them together. "There were reasons I reacted the way I did, reasons that had nothing to do with you."

"What reasons?"

How to make him understand? How to choose the right words to convey her feelings, to explain her motivations? It was so important that she succeed. The explanation she had envisioned as flowing glibly was instead spoken with nervous directness. "My own parents came from very different worlds. My mother was a wealthy debutante, from the cream of Annapolis's society. My father was a bartender who happened to be hired to work at a party celebrating my mother's twentieth birthday. They fell in love and eloped. Suffice it to say that they weren't very happy together."

She paused to sneak a look at Michael's face in the vain hope of gaging his reaction to her story. Seeing no sign of either encouragement or discouragement, she returned her gaze to the metal handcuffs. "To make a long story short, my father left when I was eight. My mother remarried, a wealthy and successful business executive this time. Someone from her own social strata. I grew up thinking that a man and a woman needed to have similar backgrounds and interests for a relationship to succeed."

A slight movement on Michael's part gave her the courage to look at him once again. "That's why I used the excuse of you being my employee as a reason not to get involved with you. Eventually I couldn't help myself and I broke my own set of rules. I ended up falling in love with you. But when you took me to see your family, without any prior warning or preparation, I panicked.

You see, your family reminded me a lot of my father's family. They never approved of my mother, and they gave her a real hard time."

Michael's face softened with what Brittany hoped was understanding. "My family gave you a hard time?"

"No, it wasn't their fault," she hastily assured him. "They were trying to be friendly. But all the" — how could she put this without being rude? — "exuberance . . . kind of got to me."

For the first time Michael actually smiled at her, even if it was ruefully. "You don't have to be polite. I know my family is pretty wild. I did try and warn you by telling you that I was the shy quiet one."

Brittany returned the smile, amplifying it tenfold. "So you did. And for once you weren't kidding." She studied his features with loving hunger. "Oh, Michael, I love you so much and I'm so sorry I panicked the way I did."

"We're still from two different worlds, you know," he reminded her roughly. "What makes you think we can make a go of it when your parents couldn't?"

"Because you and I really aren't that different when you get right down to it. We agree about the important things in life, about fidelity and integrity."

The slightest tinge of red colored his face.

"When did you discover all that?"

"I knew it all along, but I had an overdue heart-to-heart talk with my mother which helped clear my thinking. She told me that her first marriage broke up because her and my father's differences were fundamental and went far beyond the disparity in their backgrounds. It turns out that my father was actually a compulsive gambler. So all this time I've been afraid of something that was never an issue. Don't you see? I love you, Michael Devlin. I love you just the way you are. I wouldn't have you any different. But will you still have me?"

Michael didn't make any flowery replies, no impassioned declarations. But he said the one word Brittany longed to hear above all others at that moment. He said, "Yes." And then he kissed her.

Of all the kisses he'd ever given her, this one was the most special. It reflected the full spectrum of their emotions — need, relief, passion, comfort, desire, reassurance. All were different facets of love.

Their lips conversed through taste and touch. Tantalizing nibbles were used to punctuate the sensual dialogue. One kiss drifted into another in a grab-bag mixture ranging from brief tokens of affection to deep pledges of pleasure.

Brittany responded hungrily with lips that tilted and clung, and a tongue that greeted his with joyful abandon. Reality was swept away until Brittany's world contained only the man who was holding her so tightly. She pressed closer to him, chafing against the restraints placed upon her by the hand-cuffs only to realize that they were gone!

Easing away from Michael, she murmured, "How did you . . . ?"

He grinned down at her astonished face and dropped a kiss on the tip of her nose. "An old trick of the trade."

"Do you have any more tricks up your sleeve?" she asked in a seductive voice.

"A few matrimonial ones."

For a moment Brittany was speechless. "Really?" she whispered unsteadily.

"Really." Michael ran a caressing hand down her back. "Are you interested?"

"Fascinated!" Brittany melted against him and showed him exactly how fascinated she really was.

The passionately embracing couple was completely unaware of the office door opening.

Luckily, Bud caught hold of Tiffany before she entered the lovers' domain. *Well I'll be . . . wait till Arlene hears about this!* Bud thought to himself with a grin as he tried silently to urge Tiffany back out of the doorway.

The precocious kindergartner, however, refused to budge. She also refused to be silent. "Hey, everybody!" she exclaimed. "You should see what Ms. Evans and Mr. Devlin are doin' in here! It's *soooo* romantic!"

In an instant the doorway was filled with inquisitive five-year-olds. "I bet dinosaurs don't do that," Daniel stated with disapproval.

"Mmm, that's probably why they're extinct," Michael murmured against Brittany's lips before breaking off their kiss.

Reluctantly turning to face their uninvited audience, Michael and Brittany groaned when the kids started chanting, "*Sooooo rooooomantiiiic!*"

"See what you've started?" Michael accused Brittany with a rueful laugh.

To which she artfully retorted, "And aren't you glad that I did?"

He sure was!